RYKER

TITLES BY EMILY JANE TRENT

Military Romantic Suspense:

Stealth Security

Cold Peril
Lethal Peril
Ruthless Peril
Grave Peril
Deadly Peril

Must Love Danger

Hawke
Ryker
Jake

The Passion Series

Adam & Ella:

Captivated
Charmed
Cherished
Craved

Touched By You:

Dark Desire
Naked Submission
The Heart's Domination
Bound By Love
Deep Obsession
Forbidden Pleasures
Raw Burn
Desperately Entwined
Fierce Possession
Intimate Secrets
Whispered Confessions
Vivid Temptation

Sexy & Dangerous

Perfectly Shattered
Perfectly Ruined
Perfectly Flawed
Perfectly Broken

Rinaldi Romances

Gianni & Leah:

Leah's Seduction – Book 1
Leah's Seduction – Book 2
Leah's Seduction – Book 3
Leah's Seduction – Book 4
Leah's Seduction – Book 5
Leah's Seduction – Book 6
Leah's Seduction – Book 7
Leah's Seduction – Book 8
Leah's Seduction – Book 9
Leah's Seduction – Book 10

Kyra's Story

Stay With Me – Book 1: Lust
Stay With Me – Book 2: Secrets
Stay With Me – Book 3: Betrayal
Stay With Me – Book 4: Confessions

Cooper & Daniela

Daniela's Crazy Love: The Prequel
Daniela's Crazy Love: The Novel

Bend To My Will:

Forbidden Passion
Seductive Affair
Intimate Kiss
Deep Longing
Illicit Craving
Wicked Obsession
Luscious Sins
Sexy Addiction
Secret Torment
Daring Confessions
Eternal Love
Sweet Promise

Fighting For Gisele

UNLEASHED
UNTAMED
UNBROKEN
UNDEFEATED

RYKER

MUST LOVE DANGER

Emily Jane Trent

This book is a work of fiction. Names, characters, places and incidents either are the product of the author's imagination or are used fictitiously, and any resemblance to actual persons, living or dead, business establishments, events, or locales is entirely coincidental. The publisher does not have any control over and does not assume any responsibility for author or third-party websites or their content.

Ryker Copyright © 2019
by Emily Jane Trent

All rights reserved.
This book or any portion thereof may not be reproduced or used in any manner whatsoever without the express written permission of the publisher except for the use of brief quotations in a book review.

Printed in the United States of America
First Printing, 2019

ISBN: 9781086647181

Camden Lee Press, LLC
12112 N Rancho Vistoso Plaza
Suite 150-101
Oro Valley, AZ 85755

www.EmilyJaneTrent.com

ACKNOWLEDGEMENTS

No book is published in isolation. So many helped me, some in ways they never imagined. From my friends and family, my mentor, and a long list of indie authors, all have contributed to my success. Without my editor, cover artist, formatting expert, and others who played a part in making this book, I'd never be able to create these books for you like I do. I want to thank each of them for their good work.

A special thank you to all my readers: I hope you enjoy this romantic tale. It's been very rewarding to write. It's my pleasure to continue to create stories for you. I look forward to meeting you at my fan page, Emily Jane Trent Books, or at my website. My success is only because you read and enjoy these stories. I appreciate each of you.

CHAPTER 1

Mia Scott was a self-made woman. She'd seen an opportunity where only obstacles and unfairness had been before. The educational software she'd developed had the potential to aid young students with learning disabilities.

In her youth, she'd had an inability to learn and education had been a rocky road. She'd felt stupid, lost, and frustrated. But at the age of thirty-one, she was the owner of a growing tech company in Philadelphia. How that happened was the story of the year.

Her name was in the news, and tech publications raved about the potential of her new computer program. That was fortunate but came with a price. Her privacy was at a minimum. Since she was a young female entrepreneur, her photo was plastered across the media.

Wherever she went, it seemed that someone recognized her. Like a movie star, she'd started wearing dark glasses, but that did little good. She'd become a celebrity. But it couldn't be avoided. Where big money was involved, the public took notice.

Even the owner of an expanding tech company needed a break, Mia had told her team—for just a few days. Discreetly, she had her assistant book a room at a woodside resort in the Laurel Highlands, about a four-hour drive from Philly.

Mia leaned her head against the back seat, trusting her driver to get her to the sought-after destination. The brochure had boasted that it was the perfect place to get away from it all. It invitingly mentioned that a guest could be pampered at the luxury spa and engage in outdoor activities in a beautiful setting.

That was precisely what she intended to do. The stresses and pressures that came with recruiting investors for her venture had worn her down. A few days away sounded awfully good. She'd gone alone, craving downtime.

The getaway started out very promising. The resort was an English Tudor-style building, and her room was spacious with a vaulted ceiling, crystal chandeliers, and a jetted soaking tub. Mia changed clothes then went straight to the heated outdoor infinity pool.

She sank into the warm water and gazed at the view. The woodlands were lovely and the pool relaxing. A few tranquil days would calm her nerves and restore her energy. She closed her eyes and took a deep breath. For a few minutes, her life wasn't one high-pressure meeting after the other.

And there was no one around snapping her picture or peppering her with questions. She'd left the company in the capable hands of her team, managed by Iris, her closest and dearest friend. For a few hours, she didn't have to worry; she could enjoy a mini vacation.

After the pool, Mia indulged in a massage at the spa then took a nap. She couldn't believe that she'd fallen asleep in the afternoon. But she really was tired and had overextended herself for months. When she got hungry, she went to the outdoor sunset terrace restaurant and drank a glass of wine with Chilean sea bass. It was late March and the weather was pleasant.

She sipped her wine, noticing a red robin in a nearby tree—his presence a sign of spring. Then a flock of snow geese flew high overhead on their way to the tundra, a spring migration. It was quite a sight to watch. The waiter brought the dessert menu, so she made a selection.

After all, the next few days were downtime. Mia's phone hadn't vibrated with its endless messages, but only because she'd turned it off. Whatever came up could surely wait a day, or Iris could handle it. Still, it was difficult to resist checking messages.

She tried to ignore her security guys lingering

near the restaurant. The two guards had come in a separate vehicle and were under instructions to stay in the background. It wasn't a simple task for the two beefy men to appear invisible.

Mia saw them every time she turned around. But then she knew they were on the premises. The other guests didn't realize they weren't vacationers. At least they'd worn casual garb and not black suits. Yet their attitude was anything but relaxed.

That evening, Mia went to the bar to listen to live music. Already, she was wondering if she was cut out for leisure activities. There was so much to do, so much at stake. But if there was any opportunity to take a break from the onslaught of responsibilities, it was then.

Once the negotiations with investors began in earnest, taking a day off would be next to impossible. That night, Mia nestled into a plush armchair to read. She'd chosen a novel, hoping to escape into the story. Yet she found that she couldn't resist flipping through the pages of the tech magazine she'd brought.

It was hopeless. She was a workaholic. Maybe she'd go home early. Although that wouldn't do, because Iris had made her promise to stay for the entire weekend. It was useless. She slipped on her shoes to go down the hall for ice.

The machine was in an alcove by the elevator

bay. Mia went to the hotel window and looked out. Since it was dusk, she should pull the drapes. But something caught her attention. It was a black limo that looked out of place.

Oddly, she'd noticed it earlier. When she'd left the pool, the limo had driven through the parking lot. For months, she'd been followed and photographed and harassed. Mia dreaded to think that some reporter had followed her to the resort. But that made no sense. She had only told her team where she was going, and her driver had assured her that they hadn't been followed.

When she'd left the bar, her security had followed her to her room, ensuring that she got inside safely. It unnerved her to see the black limo parked below. Surely, it belonged to a guest. She shouldn't assume that everything had to do with her.

Mia wasn't going to focus on that. Once she got a bucket of ice, she was going to cool the bottle of champagne that the hotel had provided. Then she'd sip a glass to get her mind off work. She walked over to the door, but when she pulled it open, it flew back with force.

Two men in knit masks shoved her inside and bolted the door. Mia shrieked, but the sound was muffled by one man's hand. He dragged her away from the door, while the other stormed inside to look around. Terrified, Mia bit the man's hand, causing him to throw her at the wall like a sack of beans, and she fell to the floor.

Mia scrambled away, reeling from the sudden assault. She'd left the bathroom light on, which gave her an idea. In a split second, she ran for the bathroom, only a couple of feet away. Then she locked the door, still breathing hard. The tiled room was as close to a safe room as she was going to get. She moved away from the door and huddled by the bathtub. It would provide a temporary barrier if the door burst open.

She looked around, desperate for any kind of weapon. Cuticle scissors would hardly work. Although she could stab one of the men in the eye. Maybe. But that would leave the other one free to recapture her. There had to be a better option. The bathroom had no window, and she was upstairs anyway, so escape was out of the question.

Noise from the other room frightened her. She didn't know who they were or what they wanted. She needed to call for help, but her phone was in the other room. Her pulse raced as she tried to think of a way out. The intruders seemed occupied for the moment.

Mia heard them talking in a foreign language, some Baltic tongue. She had no clue what they were saying or whether they'd break down the bathroom door any second. As long as she didn't interfere, the men didn't appear concerned about her.

But that could change. And Mia had seen the flash of a gun barrel just before the brute had tossed her against the wall. She kept in shape with aerobics classes, but she was no match for two muscled men. And she hadn't handled a gun before, so even if she could grab it, it would do her little good.

Mia wished that hotel rooms weren't soundproofed, because it made it unlikely that another guest would complain about the noise—or not soon enough. If only she had her phone. But she didn't, so had to prepare in case the worst happened.

She dumped water on the tile floor by the door, so any intruder would slip upon entry. Careful to stay across the room from the water, she plugged in the hair dryer and held it in both hands like a taser. A blast of hot air in the eyes would slow down an attacker. But then what?

Mia had no idea. She'd have to make a run for it. After sliding through the water, she'd have to race for the door then out to the hall, hoping someone would be around. Where were her security guards when she needed them?

Through her life, Mia had witnessed, even experienced, brutality. But she couldn't recall a time when she'd been attacked by strangers. Before it had been someone she knew, a person who she knew was prone to violence.

Yet she hadn't seen this coming. Her sole focus was to get out alive. Whatever the men wanted, they could take. She had some cash in her purse, so hoped they'd find it and be satisfied. Outside the bathroom door, it sounded like a wild party.

Then it went silent.

Mia held her breath. Could it be? Had the men left?

She wasn't quick to assume they had. Quietly, she crept toward the door, with the hairdryer still in hand. Leaning against the cool wood panel, she tried to tell if there was anyone on the other side. But there was no talking or other noise.

Her pulse still pounded, as she dared hope that it was over. It was too soon to open the door. The men might be waiting on the other side. It could be a ploy to get her to open the door, easier than breaking it down.

Mia waited, then waited longer. She couldn't take it. She had to get out of that room and get help. It had been long enough. Holding on to the hairdryer, she unlocked the door. The cord wasn't long enough to keep it plugged in, but she could certainly knock one of them on the head with it.

Mia opened the door and gazed into her room. No one else was there. Cautiously stepping out, she looked around. The place was trashed. It was baffling, as she couldn't imagine why it had happened.

Coming to her senses, she grabbed the hotel phone and dialed the desk. Nearly incoherent, she babbled something about being attacked. Within minutes, there was a pounding at the door, startling her. "Security."

Mia opened the door, and hotel security entered. She slumped into a chair, trembling. Somehow, she managed to tell the guard what had occurred. It sounded like an unbelievable story, even as she recounted the highlights.

The guard spoke to someone on his phone, and more personnel appeared. The concierge asked if he should call for medical help, but Mia shook her head. Amazingly, she wasn't injured. The question was: what had prompted the attack?

Mia stared, unsure how to respond. She vaguely wondered when her security would arrive on the scene. As if hearing her thoughts, her two security men walked in, appearing to have hastily thrown on shirts and pants without bothering to comb their messy hair. She was glad that *someone* had been able to sleep.

"Mia, are you okay?" Her tall security guard looked concerned.

It wasn't good enough. She paid a lot of money for protection. "I was robbed at gunpoint. And where were you? I thought you had it all under control, that I was safe."

"You told us to stay in the shadows."

"Yes, but not literally." Mia glared at him. "I just meant... Oh, God. If I have to explain it, then what's the use?" She waved a hand. "You're fired." Then she looked at her other security guard. "And you too."

Her security looked at her but offered no argument.

"I'll call and arrange transport home," Mia said. "Just go."

The concierge gave her a tiny bow. "At your service, Ms. Scott. May I move you to another room, while we..." He looked at the mess.

"Yes, and make it one at lobby level, near security, please."

Mia was about to leave when law enforcement entered and addressed her. She wasn't going to catch a break.

After a forty-minute interview, the cops determined that three hundred dollars in cash had been stolen, along with her laptop and phone.

"Did you have any jewelry?" one of the cops said.

Mia shook her head.

"Anything in the safe?"

"No, I'm on a short holiday. I didn't bring much."

The police seemed as baffled as she was. "You're in the public eye a lot, Ms. Scott. It wouldn't be too hard to find out where you were staying."

"Apparently not."

"But you didn't have much to steal, and the intruders didn't harm you...fortunately."

Mia had some ideas; she knew more about her company and what a thief might want from her. But she saw no reason to tell the local police. It was only a hunch, anyway.

*****

Once Mia was secure in a different room, a suite provided by the hotel at no charge, she used the hotel phone to call her best friend. Iris Bancroft had been by her side through many ups and downs. This one took the cake.

She'd met Iris in grade school, and they had instantly bonded. Although Mia hadn't gone to college like her friend had, she'd ended up in the field of technology and started a business with Iris. There was no one better to establish a start-up with than her, a woman Mia would trust with her life.

It was the middle of the night, but Mia couldn't wait. She needed to hear a friendly voice, had to process the trauma. "Iris...it's me."

"Mia?" There was a rustling sound. "What time is it?"

"You don't want to know. And I wouldn't call at this hour if it wasn't important." Mia launched into a description of events—disbelieving that it had actually happened even as she was telling the story.

"Are you thinking what I'm thinking?" Iris said.

"Yep, you read my mind. The thieves were after whatever was on my laptop."

"Couldn't they just have swiped it while you were entering the hotel? You know, like purse snatchers?"

Mia sighed. "Whoever it was wished to make a point."

"Yeah...you're vulnerable," Iris said, "and thanks to your own security crew, no less. Don't you worry. I'll have an escort there for you, before breakfast...which isn't far off."

"You're a true friend."

Mia tried to get a couple of hours of sleep, but it was futile. She was too upset. Instead, she paced the floor, fuming. She was tempted to call her manager in the middle of the night, too. But Griffen LaMont was a married man and his wife wouldn't appreciate that.

He was a loyal team member and managed the company's affairs in a variety of ways. She counted on him. It wasn't his fault that some idiots had pursued her. But she was still mad. When the sun came up at last, she downed a cup of coffee then made the call.

"You what?" Griffen said, in his normally calm

voice.

"Don't say that like I just told you I misplaced my luggage," Mia said. "The security you sent to protect me botched the job."

Griffen was quiet.

"I was scared out of my mind, and alone." Mia expelled a breath. "I lost an expensive laptop. And I could have been *killed*."

"I'm so sorry, Mia. I really am," Griffen said. "You did the right thing by firing them. If you hadn't, I would have."

"Who hired them in the first place? I cannot tolerate such incompetence."

"Those two had been with us for a while," Griffen said. "I suppose this is the first time they had really been put to the test. And who hired them? That honor goes to your ex-husband."

"Goddammit." Mia rubbed her temple. "Didn't we clean things out when I divorced him two years ago?"

"I thought so, but it didn't occur to me that security was lacking."

"I certainly hope it has now," Mia said. "Things are only getting to get more intense as we move forward with investors. I can't afford an incident. And for that matter, you'll need to keep this quiet. Having the company owner's life in peril tends to make investors nervous."

"You are absolutely right," Griffen said. "I'm

sure Iris is all over that, handling any leaks. And I have a connection in the police force. I'll lean on him."

"And who is that?"

"Lonnie, an old friend of mine. And his cousin Ryker is an ex-SEAL, who owns an executive protection firm," Griffen said. "I'll give him a buzz and see what I can set up."

"Whoever this *Ryker* is, and his protection firm…just make sure they know their job, understood?"

Mia wasn't at all reassured. She was furious and not calming down. It went beyond her own personal safety. Much more was at stake. She'd worked for years to get to the point where she was now. Her company was about to take on major investors.

It wasn't about the money, either. Sure, it was a good thing. She wouldn't turn it away. But it was so much more than that. It was about the kids who needed the educational software she'd developed. Kids who had issues with learning, who faced an uncertain future unless they could cope. Kids not much different than her, with a disability she was all too familiar with. She couldn't allow this chance to be snatched away—not when success was so close. She couldn't afford any mistakes. It was imperative that she get back to Philly safely and see this through.

CHAPTER 2

Ryker Johnson was on duty that weekend. He was used to extended schedules, and the executive protection business required it. Since he'd founded Black Swan Protection with Hawke, he'd worked all kinds of hours.

Jonathan Hawkins Turner was a guy to trust, particularly as a business partner. As they'd been on numerous deployments together as Navy SEALs, the bond was tight. Since retiring over a year ago, Ryker had teamed up with his buddy to use his hard-earned skills in the civilian sector.

The Black Swan team had learned to be alert for the unexpected, events like the appearance of black swans—the events they cared about only involved danger. There was one rule for taking on new teammates and it was stated in the application: *Must Love Danger*.

That described Ryker, as well as Hawke and other former military who had joined the team. The company had grown, as executive protection was in demand.

Leaning back in his chair, Ryker studied a

photograph of a woman—a very beautiful and famous woman.

Hawke strolled by the desk. "I see you got the profile data on the new case."

"This is the client, Mia Scott...the owner of Mental Magic?" Ryker stared at the picture. "This is going to be a bitch. Haven't you read about her? She's a prima donna, difficult to deal with."

"It's our job," Hawke said. "Besides, I think she has a right to be demanding, considering her position."

"You take the client, then."

"No can do," Hawke said. "The client is expecting us this afternoon, so she's all yours. It's the weekend. Emilia has been working long hours at the lab, and I promised her a day alone...movies, dinner."

"You sound like a married man."

"Almost," Hawke said. "Maddie got all the preliminaries on the intake form, and Jake has researched the background, including details of her former security team's actions. He'll go over it with you."

Ryker clicked to the file on his computer and scanned the background report. Then he went to have a chat with Jake to gain more insight. He had a feeling he was going to need all the support he could get. But he'd deal with the case. There was no way he couldn't handle a woman, no matter her high opinion of herself.

Jake Holland was in charge of digital security. The guy was a pro and had years of experience from his Navy career. Often, what he was able to uncover was impressive. But Jake wasn't at his desk.

Ryker waved the photo in front of Amanda, Jake's co-conspirator in computer hacking. "You know about this?" He could tell from the gleam in her eye that she not only knew, but had contributed to the revelatory information in the report.

Amanda had her fiery red hair twisted up on her head. Her blue eyes flared. "You got a problem with that?" It was just like her to attack first. She was ex-military with attitude, had been in the Air Force.

Ryker didn't know what the chip on her shoulder was, but he was about to get a piece of her mind. He could tell by the look in her eyes. "I've seen that expression before. Go ahead, spit it out."

"Mia Scott started her company from her own savings. She's a visionary, focused and passionate," Amanda said.

"You sound like a groupie."

"Don't get smart. I'm serious here," Amanda said. "She's trying to do a good thing, and I suggest that before you meet with her, you take five minutes of your precious time to find out what Mental Magic is all about."

"Is that an order?"

Amanda smirked. "Call it a suggestion. Anyway, her security screwed up big time, as I'm sure you could tell from my report."

Now it was *her* report. "I got that much," Ryker said. "I read what Jake found out when he spoke to her manager. With all the mistakes her security made, I can't fathom how they got hired in the first place."

Amanda proceeded to give him an earful. She enlightened him on her knowledge of the new tech company, what was going on, and what was involved. She ended, "Mia Scott's security matters. Don't blow it." Then she went back to work.

*****

Mental Magic's headquarters was in one of the state-of-the-art buildings in downtown Philly. It towered above Penn Landing with a view of the Delaware River. In Ryker's opinion, it was pretentious. And what kind of a name was that, anyway? No serious investor would plunk down money for a start-up that sounded like a child's game.

Inside, the building was all glass and chrome, with expansive windows offering views of the city's skyscrapers. The polished floors gleamed, and the employees were dressed as if ready for a photoshoot. Ryker had worn a clean shirt with slacks, not jeans.

But no way was he showing up in a suit and tie. The job didn't require it. If Ms. Scott wanted security, she'd have the best—dress codes aside. He confidently strode toward the elevator bay, prepared to take charge of security in the most efficient way possible.

Ryker was expected, so the receptionist buzzed him in right away. He'd anticipated meeting with her manager, but was told that Ms. Scott wished to make her own decisions concerning security. He tapped on the door.

"Please come in."

It took Ryker a moment to take in the scene. He'd known what to expect, since he'd seen her photograph. But Mia Scott was more stunning in person. She exuded charisma that didn't show in a picture. Her smile was warm, but the look in her eyes was wary.

"Ryker," she said, and shook his hand. "Please have a seat. I believe we have some matters to discuss." The way she spoke told him that she was up to speed. She knew who he was and most likely had looked into his company.

Mia's dark blond hair was shaped in a trendy cut. Her brown eyes were large and expressive, revealing more knowledge and experience than he'd expected. She was the prominent owner of a tech company, and a woman at that.

As if that wasn't enough, Mia was the poster child for sexiness. She had beautiful, perfect lips, with flawless skin and a fit, toned body. Ryker noted how her filmy top and pencil skirt clung to her curves. The blouse was flesh-toned, revealing little but encouraging the imagination to conjure up much more.

"I see that you work out," Ryker said, then kicked himself. What a lame thing to say.

Mia smiled, without faltering or losing her cool. "I've been known to." Her gaze roamed over his muscled physique, making Ryker glad that he stayed in shape. "I'm sure you do too. But then, you're ex-military, so I'd expect no less."

It was time to change the dynamics. Ryker sat across from her, shoulders squared, back straight. "It seems that you require a new protection team."

Mia studied him, apparently in no rush to agree. She narrowed her eyes. "And why should I trust you?"

Ryker wasn't in the habit of defending himself or his team. He didn't intend to start now. The way Mia carried herself, her attitude, and even how she looked spoke volumes. She was ego-driven, a personality type that he was familiar with.

Mia struck him as an ungrateful woman. For all her success, she persisted in looking down on others. Her question didn't deserve an answer. "If you expect us to handle you with kid gloves, then this won't work."

Ryker would gladly dump her and move on to his next assignment. All she had to do was say the word. But he couldn't walk away unless she did; that would violate his code. He wouldn't abandon an innocent, or a woman in need of protection.

To her credit, Mia didn't flinch at his challenge. "Tell me your take on this situation."

"Your security was faulty," Ryker said.

"So I discovered."

"And not just that." Ryker leaned forward. "New security measures are needed to ensure your safety."

Mia listened without interrupting.

"I'll inspect your circle of influence, meaning those closest to you," Ryker said. "It's clear that there was a lack of vetting before hiring. It's imprudent to allow untested individuals to have access to you or your company. In a crisis, such individuals might fail in their duties...or worse."

"And you are better?"

"If I wasn't and I didn't have the team to back me up, I wouldn't accept the responsibility." Ryker sensed that she was open to what he had to say. "For starters, taking your laptop and phone with you to a public hotel isn't advisable."

Mia's nostrils flared. "I'm not *stupid*. My security guards may have been bumbling idiots, but I'm not. The laptop I had with me was merely for convenience. It had been cleaned out and purged of all password information. And the phone was a burner."

It was good to know he was dealing with a woman who had some brains. "You locked yourself in the bathroom when the attackers forced their way in?"

"Yes, I had to do something."

"Actually, that's pretty good," Ryker said. "But the intruders were still in the other room. How did you plan to defend yourself?"

Mia didn't reply, but she had a sheepish expression.

"That's what I thought," Ryker said. "Self-defense measures can save your life. Security won't always be nearby. I'll arrange some practice sessions for you."

Ryker was used to being assertive and taking control. It was his nature, and it was how he'd been trained. Clients usually appreciated that attitude and preferred to be taken care of.

Mia pointed her finger at him. "You're bossy, and that doesn't work with me. You're on my team, not the other way around."

What was going on? Ryker was expected to

protect her but not take charge. He flashed to his marriage. His young wife had died while he was away on deployment. He'd loved her beyond comprehension. Had he been bossy...controlling? She hadn't complained about it if he had.

A fist tightened around his heart at thoughts of his young love. Ryker wasn't sure he'd ever get over losing her. He wasn't sure he wanted to. He shoved the memories back down.

"How did the attackers know where I was staying?" Mia said, pulling his attention back to the present.

"Social media, messages your team sent to each other."

"But those are private," Mia said.

"Guess not." Ryker noted the surprised look she gave him. "We live in the information age. It's best not to text on a phone connected to a public network. And for privacy, I recommend using a fake email address. Digital security is a big deal and is key to keeping you safe."

Mia offered no argument, apparently impressed with his knowledge and expertise. Maybe Ryker could instill confidence in his company after all. "My team will protect you. We have two digital security experts on our staff, and are prepared for any eventuality." Ryker gave her a moment to consider that. "We can do our job, but only if you cooperate."

For some reason, Mia didn't look cooperative. But Ryker intended to establish her security the right way this time. No more *buddy guards*; it was professional protection all the way. He'd gone over what he needed to in the first meeting.

Ryker got up to leave. "And for the record, it's a bad idea to use security hired by your ex-husband." He knew that Hawke would give him hell for antagonizing the client. But he couldn't help it; the woman was infuriating.

"Anything else?" Mia said curtly.

When Ryker shook his head, she motioned toward the door—his cue to leave.

CHAPTER 3

Mia stared at the door after it shut behind Ryker. As if she didn't have enough problems, she had to deal with an arrogant alpha type. He thought he could run the show, order her about, and knew more than she did.

It was frustrating to have to depend on others for her safety. In her youth, she'd had no one to count on, so had learned to do things herself. Iris had been Mia's only friend through the toughest challenges, and still was the best friend a woman could ask for.

But as far as male role models, Mia's parents had died when she was a toddler—from drug overdoses, she later learned. It hadn't been the best way to start life, having addicts for parents.

Mia had been so young when they died that their lack of parenting skills hadn't affected her. But she certainly had no father figure. Foster care had involved moving from one home to another, and she hadn't had the chance to bond.

Her only solace had been staying over with Iris sometimes, whose parents were gems. If only Mia had been that lucky. She didn't feel sorry for herself; there hadn't been time for that. To survive she'd had to hustle, in one way or another.

If Ryker thought he could prance into her office and tell her how to manage things, he was wrong. Mia might allow him to handle her protection as long as he didn't overstep boundaries—which she'd soon make clear to him.

That Ryker was eye candy didn't help matters. Mia reflected on the memory of his chiseled form. He was muscled and honed to perfection. When he'd entered and looked at her, Mia nearly melted.

So what if his blue-gray eyes had penetrated deep to her soul? So what if he had short hair that she itched to run her palm over? And it didn't make a bit of difference that he looked drool-worthy in that dress shirt that fit like it had been tailored to his Adonis body.

One thing that absolutely wasn't going to happen was giving in to the powerful attraction. Mia was a warm-blooded woman. There was no way to notice Ryker's good looks and not be affected. But she wouldn't act on it—not on her life.

It hadn't been that many years ago that she'd swooned for a handsome man, only to end up marrying him. James Walsh was attractive, but mean-tempered. He was seven years older than she was, and his age had promised maturity and experience.

Mia had been wrong. After a whirlwind courtship, and a wedding before she'd known him a year, his real personality had been revealed. In the beginning, he'd appeared romantic, and did all the right things. But it was a façade.

In reality, James lacked social skills. He was controlling and possessive. What started as heated arguments rapidly became mental and physical abuse. Mia was familiar with abuse, having suffered much during her growing years.

She couldn't believe that she'd stepped into such a relationship. She chastised herself for being naïve, which seemed impossible, considering that she'd been mistreated so often before.

James would build her up, just to tear her down. It was done in a manner that had been difficult to spot. But when he felt safe enough to physically enforce his will, Mia put a stop to it. She divorced him and didn't look back.

There was no way in hell that she was going to hook up with another controlling male. It just wasn't going to happen. She was still trying to escape from the last man who'd swept her off her feet with his take-charge attitude.

There was a knock at her door, then Iris walked in. "Wow, was that buff guy your new security detail?"

"Iris, don't start," Mia said. "You know I've sworn off men. I don't care if he's the heartthrob of the century—all I want is for him to do his job."

"Yeah, I know." Iris ran her fingertips through her short, dark hair, then plopped into the chair. She was petite, and sometimes in business environments she was underestimated. But Mia had known her since she was a kid. Iris was one person to rely on, and when she looked at a person with those lovely brown eyes of hers, she saw right through any pretense.

"Okay, so I noticed Ryker's good looks, but that's where it ends."

"You've hired Black Swan to handle your protection?" Iris said. "According to Griffen, the employees are ex-military and have a stellar reputation."

"We'll see," Mia said. "I've hired the company, but I have my eye on them. Any screwups and they'll be gone."

"Agreed."

"Were you able to snuff out that robbery story?" Mia said. "I'd rather not have that leak to the media."

Iris shook her head. "I couldn't do it. It seems whoever orchestrated that incident wants to make a point...virally."

"You've got to be kidding? It went viral already?"

"You are a celebrity, you know," Iris said. "You're like a diva or something. The public hangs on every word you say, everything you do."

"I wanted my software to catch on, but I don't get the allure about my private life," Mia said.

"That's how it works. You do something noteworthy and word spreads," Iris said. "And if you happen to be a gorgeous young woman who is the owner of a multimillion-dollar tech company, then your privacy is a thing of the past."

"Next I'll be checking out at the grocery store and see my picture plastered on one of those gossip rags."

Iris shrugged. "It already is."

"Can we change the subject?" Mia was nervous. Large investments had been made in her company and it all rested on her shoulders. But she hadn't been able to trust her own security. The more famous she became, the more vulnerable she was.

Iris went to get a glass of water from the side table. "What are those?" She motioned toward a huge flower arrangement.

"Flowers."

"Yeah, I can see that. But how did they get here?"

Mia sighed. "It seems my ex-husband is making a plea to get back together."

Iris plucked a red rose from the vase and put it

up to her nose. "Has he lost his mind?"

"I'm sure that happened a long time ago," Mia said. "James has been after me ever since the day I kicked him out."

"I can hear him saying, *I'm sorry, we can work it out*...like you'd really fall for that."

"You know about the emails, love letters, texts, and even the begging for dinner dates, but..."

"Let me guess," Iris said. "The divorce is final next month, so this is his last-ditch effort to get you back."

"I think so," Mia said. "It's annoying. I just want him to go away. I have too much to deal with."

"Speaking of which...I'm afraid our investors will be shaken to hear that you were threatened at gunpoint," Iris said. "I'll set up a meeting with Griffen and the team. We need to strategize."

"I'd like to know who wanted my laptop."

"Could be someone who isn't anxious for Mental Magic to succeed," Iris said. "But it's difficult to imagine who would be against developing the software. It will change education for the better. Who wouldn't want that?"

"The world isn't like that," Mia said. "You've known me longer than anyone. You know what I've been through, and even what *you've* been through as part of my team. Not everyone is on our side."

Iris left to set up the meeting, and Mia stared at the colorful flowers. She couldn't stand the sight of them, didn't want them there. The display reminded her of James, of the fights, the anger, the bruises. She'd been married to him for a year, then separated for two years.

Most of those years had been filled with drama. Mia had gotten out of a damaging marriage, but not nearly soon enough. She shouldn't have dated James to start with. Reflecting on all the signs that were there, she couldn't believe she hadn't put a stop to it sooner.

Mia shuddered. Her ex-husband had been overbearing and demeaning toward her. When she threatened to leave, he was sorry—until the next time. The divorce would soon be final, then he'd leave her alone for good.

*****

The Mental Magic staff huddled together in the conference room. Griffen ran the meeting, and Iris took notes. It was agreed that whoever stole Mia's laptop had hoped to gain access to the proprietary program or confidential information.

The thieves could have been hired by a competitor, but if so, that was the first indication that the competition was playing dirty. With the notoriety Mia had achieved, the act could have been from the public sector. Maybe it was a jealous fan, or a simple criminal act.

Instead of dwelling on the mystery, Mia informed her crew that a new executive protection team had been hired. Black Swan would send protection agents to the office to arrange tighter security. Each team member would be clued in on new procedures.

It was the best she could do. Mia might have her doubts, since the new company was unproven. But it was her best option. She needed to strengthen her inner circle. One attack was sufficient to make the point that she had vulnerabilities.

After years of investors passing on Mia's business plan, she and her team finally had the financing to move ahead. With each refusal, she'd regrouped, made improvements and resubmitted her requests. She'd found new investors and hadn't given up.

Now it was finally going to pay off. The last thing the team needed was for their investors to lose faith. Having come this far, Mia couldn't let everyone down, least of all the school kids who stood to benefit the most—kids she knew and cared about.

The meeting ended with Griffen stating that he would oversee the protection arrangements and ensure the procedure went smoothly for the staff. Mia continued with her day, swamped with emails that had piled up, plus a few urgent messages.

Mia had no dinner plans and preferred going straight home. Soaking in a warm bath and listening to music sounded better than going out. She let reception know that she was gone for the day, then took the elevator to the parking garage.

One luxury Mia had allowed herself was a metallic-blue Audi. She'd driven plenty of beater cars in her time, so when her salary warranted the expenditure, she'd splurged. The car was a kick to drive, and she liked cruising home with the music cranked up. She'd paid extra for quality speakers.

With her purse over her shoulder, Mia strolled through the lot and spotted her vehicle. She grabbed her key fob then stopped. A man moved from behind the car to stand by the driver's side door. It was James.

Mia's nerves were frazzled; she didn't need to have a conversation with him.

James was dressed in a white shirt with the top buttons open and a scarf around his neck. His attempt to look cool fell flat. His dark, wavy hair was fashionably messy, and his gray slacks suitably creased. But the look of contempt in his icy blue eyes negated any friendliness.

The sight of him riddled her stomach with anxiety. The fear of what he might do made her want to turn and run. But she refused to let him have the upper hand. He'd intimidated her for far too long. She dug deep for strength, refusing to let him see the effect he had on her.

"Did you get the flowers?" James said.

Even his deep, raspy voice grated on her. He had thick brows and eyes that were too close together. Mia wondered how she'd ever thought he was handsome. There was a menacing quality about him, one that she should have spotted when she met him.

"Don't send me flowers, James. Don't send me anything. No cards, no letters, no emails, no texts." Mia glared at him. "Have I made my point?"

"I just want to talk with you," James said. "We were married, lived as husband and wife. Surely, you can't throw that away."

"You threw that away, with your mistreatment, with your anger, and your..." Mia expelled a breath. "I have bigger problems than you. Let me get into my car and go."

"Yes, I know about your bigger problems. I watch social media like anyone else," James said. "I could help you. I could pull some strings."

Mia had made a mistake hooking up with him, because he was an abusive ass. But the bigger mistake in judgement had been to hook up with an ass who happened to have clout with the Board of Education. "Help me, like you did last time? By lying about me to the board?"

James moved closer, and Mia flinched. "I didn't mean that. I was angry. You made me angry."

"No, James. That's not how it works. You don't get to put that on me," Mia said. "Your anger is your issue, not mine. I'm not part of your life anymore, and in a month, all legal ties will be severed."

Fury flashed in his eyes, just before he grabbed her arm. "You're making a mistake." He yanked her, but then a voice stopped him.

"I'd let her go if I were you."

Mia looked up to see a tall, lean guy in a cotton shirt. His dark, spiky hair and brown eyes gave him a ruggedly handsome look. He had a square jaw, broad shoulders, and a calm assurance that gave James pause, so he let her go.

Then the guy flashed a killer smile. "That's better." He looked at Mia. "Are you okay?"

Mia nodded.

"Be on your way," the man said to James. "I don't want to have to say it twice." The man focused on Mia, clearly assuming that her attacker would heed the command to leave. "I should introduce myself. My name is Caleb Rowe."

"Well, you showed up at the right time," Mia said.

"I've been watching."

Great, now Mia had a new stalker. As if her ex-husband wasn't enough.

"Ryker has set up security for you, and I'm your close protection. I didn't want to be intrusive, so I wouldn't have acted unless necessary."

"You're with Black Swan?"

"Yes, ma'am. And you can relax; there is a team assigned to you," Caleb said. "You have my assurance on that."

"You're going to continue hanging around me?"

Caleb shined that winning smile on her. "I believe so."

Mia leaned against the car, relieved and exasperated. Couldn't she have been informed beforehand?

"You have Ryker's card and can call if you need to," Caleb said, then handed her a phone. "This is a safe phone, the one you should use for any important conversations. The team will set up a discreet email for you and ensure that your communications are encrypted."

"Can I go now?"

"Absolutely, ma'am. You're in charge."

You wouldn't know it—from what Mia could tell, Ryker ran things now. "How long have you been here?"

"I was sent as soon as your manager called for

security, making it clear that it was urgent," Caleb said. "I understood that your former team was relieved of their duties."

"You seem to know an awful lot," Mia said. "Am I to understand that you were protecting me even before Ryker arrived?"

"That is true," Caleb said. "And the team."

Mia glanced around, sure that the teammates wouldn't be visible to her. She caught on quickly, and that was part of the deal. If she didn't know they were there, then any unfriendly presence wouldn't either—just as James hadn't.

"I'm going home now," Mia said. "I assume you're going to follow me?"

"I'll be right behind you."

Once Mia was inside her Audi, she locked the doors and leaned against the headrest. Her emotions were frayed, and Ryker wasn't helping. He didn't know how to *ask* for anything. Dammit, couldn't he have consulted her before sending out his team? But no, he just went right ahead, doing what he wished.

Mia should have been grateful, not resentful. She'd navigated her life on her own so far. She didn't need some alpha male calling the shots. She was relieved that James had been scared off. God only knew how far he would have taken the encounter.

It drove home the point that James wasn't

going to back off. He wanted her to cancel the divorce. He believed they could reconcile. He lived in a fantasy world. What part of hating him didn't he get?

Considering the violent tendencies that James had exhibited—on too many occasions to count—Mia required protection. Ryker and his team were her best option. She needed them nearby to make sure no harm came to her.

But Mia didn't trust Ryker—not yet. And whether she did depended on how he behaved. If he got too pushy, she would replace him. His company wasn't the only one in Philly. He'd better watch it. She was fed up with bullying.

CHAPTER 4

Over the next few days, Ryker made sure that security was in place. The team ran countersurveillance to determine the threat level and ensure that no one unfriendly had access to Mia or her company. Other than her fans pressing in to get a better look, it had been quiet.

Caleb and his guys stuck close to Mia, just in case. Her ex-husband showing up uninvited annoyed Ryker. He didn't like to see a woman harassed, and the report of her ex grabbing her arm rubbed him the wrong way.

Further background research was done on Mental Magic and its high-profile owner. Ryker was at headquarters, anxious to find out what had been discovered. He'd read the reports in the file, but wanted to dig deeper.

Ryker looked over to see Hawke on the phone. He could hear that he was talking to Emilia, his new girlfriend. Bad time to interrupt. So Ryker cruised over to Jake's office, which was better anyway. He'd get the story straight from the researcher.

Jake was engrossed in paperwork. He rubbed his close-shaved beard then rocked back in his chair. Ryker sat across from him. "Got a minute?"

"Sure, what's up?" Jake's gray eyes were the color of steel. He had a gaze that could give an enemy pause, and had, many times. Ryker could attest to that. He was a guy that would watch your back, and a valuable teammate.

"Talk to me about Mia Scott."

"I'm sure you read the report."

"Yes," Ryker said. "Raised in foster care, had learning issues...and recently, a messy divorce."

"Yep, the learning issues are well known. It's in her public bio," Jake said. "In fact, it's her company's story and has won the public's heart. This software she's created is designed to assist with learning disabilities."

"I don't like the fact that James Walsh is harassing her."

"Yeah, her ex," Jake said. "He's a piece of work. I didn't find any police reports of the abuse, so Mia must not have gone to the authorities. But from what we gleaned from those close to her, the dude roughed her up."

Ryker clenched his fists. "That's the worst kind, a man who would do that. What's his deal?"

"That's where it gets interesting," Jake said. "He's on the Board of Education, and I can see issues with that. This new software is targeted for schools, to help kids in remedial programs. But..."

"It presents a problem when your ex is on the board," Ryker said. "That group isn't easy to deal with, anyway. Even back when I was in school, they weren't amenable toward new technologies—preferred the traditional ways."

"Yet the system leaves kids behind." Jake said. "If they can't learn with the methods offered, they are out of luck."

The more Ryker heard about James Walsh, the more he disliked him. It didn't matter that he had a respectable job; stalkers could be found in any career field. The behavior patterns were the same.

Ryker had done a bit of research on his own. Sending boxes of candy, clothing, or flowers was standard. The stalker would even show up at the victim's house, put items in the mailbox, notes on the car, and more. Asking the person to stop did no good.

Sometimes that was as far as it went. The stalker might be basically harmless, like a fan who followed a rock star around. But Ryker had told Caleb to keep an eye on Mia's ex. He didn't trust him. Especially not after hearing that the marriage had been abusive.

Ryker told Jake to see what dirt he could dig up on James Walsh, as he figured there had to be something. A guy like that probably didn't have a clean history. In dealing with a stalker, it was important to know his earlier patterns.

Mia was scheduled for self-defense sessions, and Ryker had decided to handle her training. There were classes for women available in Philly, but he preferred to provide the lessons personally. He had to make sure it was done right, and to see that she could defend herself.

That shouldn't occur, so long as his company was protecting her. But she'd been volatile when he'd met her, so might get rid of Black Swan as fast as she'd hired them. And she'd need some way to protect herself, even if from an irate ex-husband.

After hearing more of Mia's background, Ryker decided that he might have been too hard on her. She'd called him bossy, and maybe he was. He thought of his wife Amy, and how well they'd gotten along. She hadn't complained about his behavior, even though he'd been married to her for five years.

Surely, if Ryker had been that much of a pain, it would have come up. But Mia and Amy had different personalities. His wife had been a lovely woman, inside and out. She'd been caring and strong, but not aggressive or challenging.

Ryker guessed that made sense, as she had been raised in suburbia so hadn't experienced things that Mia must have. He thought of his wife, and his gut tightened. The guilt was still there. He should have been home when she died. Instead, he was on deployment and didn't even hear about her death until days after.

A workout room at the company's training center had been reserved for the session. Since Ryker was late, he jogged over. Mia should be there. She'd told him that her driver would have her there as scheduled, and she seemed like the type to be prompt.

The second time he met Mia, her effect on him was just as strong. She'd already suited up in stretch pants with a tight top. The outfit was color-coordinated; the pants had gold stripes that matched the gold top. And she was barefoot.

Good Lord, how was he going to deal with this? He'd made the wrong decision and should have let Caleb or one of the others handle Mia's training.

Her stylish hair was in a headband and she was makeup-free. The natural look suited Mia. She was as attractive in a few stretchy items of clothing as she had been in designer attire. Makeup was unnecessary. Her brown eyes were beautiful, her lips full. She didn't need to create illusions; she was a natural beauty.

Ryker walked over, making his best effort to be casual. He made a point not to stare, although that was difficult. "Good morning, Ms. Scott."

"It's Mia. We can't be formal if we're going to

wrestle each other on this mat."

"All right, *Mia*, then." Ryker already sounded like a lovesick schoolboy. He had to get it together.

Ryker proceeded. "Remember to be loud to intimidate your attacker and draw attention, in case someone is nearby that can assist you." Then he showed her how to deliver a groin kick with enough force to paralyze an attacker.

There were several variations of an elbow strike, so Ryker went through each one. Mia learned quickly. She was agile, fluid in her motions, and smart. When she caught on to a few basic moves, Ryker showed her how to escape if an attacker trapped her arms, so she couldn't move freely.

Ryker took the attacker's stance and wrapped his arms around her. The scent of her floral perfume created a physical reaction deep in his core. Maybe she could fell an opponent with sheer femininity. He shook off that thought then got back to business.

He held her, noticing how good she felt in his embrace. Mia was in shape and toned in the right places, yet, holding her close, he couldn't ignore her womanly curves. When she turned to look at him, her hair brushed his chin, making him want to dig his hands in it.

"Am I doing this right?" Mia said. She'd

brought her hands up, then held them tight to her chest so she could turn.

Ryker looked at her perfect lips, wanting to kiss her. "Yes, sure. Let's try it again."

Escaping from a headlock was a little trickier, so Ryker saved that for the next session. "Once you escape," he said, "don't go home or turn away from crowds. Walk into a well-lit store or coffee shop and call the police. And carry some sort of weapon."

"Will a lipstick taser do?" Mia said.

"I see you're one step ahead of me." Too bad her purse hadn't been accessible at that resort, or the robbery story would have had a different ending. "A taser will do the trick."

Ryker wasn't anxious to send Mia on her way. She intrigued him, so he said, "That was a good session. I'll take you for lunch. You've earned it."

Mia hesitated but didn't refuse. "Okay, I'll get cleaned up. You pick the place. I'm not familiar with restaurants around here."

Since Ryker was in jeans and a t-shirt, he opted for a casual place. Mia returned from the locker room wearing white jeans, a sweater, and ankle boots. It didn't matter what she wore—she was stunning. "You look nice."

Mia smiled, exhibiting no animosity. Whatever she had against him at the start seemed to have abated, at least for the time being. Ryker was too sharp to assume that she wouldn't bite his head off again if he annoyed her. Maybe he could get through lunch without doing so.

"Where are we going?"

"There's a café that's not far," Ryker said. "It's casual, but the food is good." He decided that there was more to Mia than he'd thought. She had a fire inside that he admired. She'd clearly had to fight for success, even her own survival. That type of grit got his attention.

The café was busy, but Ryker managed to get a table at the back. There was a window but not much of a view. It wasn't meant to be a romantic date, anyway. This was just lunch, so he could get to know the client better.

He almost believed that.

The lunch menu offered the usual fare of soups, sandwiches, and salads. Mia chose the turkey club and iced tea, while Ryker ordered pastrami on rye with a Coke. He was enjoying her company, and nearly relaxed. But he dared not get complacent.

The tone could shift without warning; he knew that much about women, and figured that was even truer with Mia. She seemed willing to talk about her software company, and he was content to listen.

"Diversity in the workplace is the current buzzword," Mia said. "But the inclusion of women within the tech field has been disappointingly slow. I'm a woman in a man's field, or so it's often thought. I had more strikes against me than just trying to fund a new, untried software program."

"You've done well."

"I started the company with my savings, and my friend Iris invested," Mia said. "That's how I got going. It's taken a long time to get this far, but now we have some serious investors."

"Where there's big money to be made or lost, there's substantial risk," Ryker said, glad that she'd hired his company for protection. Success could be a magnet for trouble.

Mia sipped her tea, and for a few minutes focused on eating. Ryker liked to watch her. There was something about her attitude, her confidence that he perceived was hard-won. She hadn't come from wealthy parents or a pampered background, yet she'd created one of the most talked-about tech companies within the past couple of years.

Since Mia wasn't being defensive, it was probably safe to ask questions. "What is the software that you created?"

"It's a learning program, but not like any you've seen." Mia shoved her plate aside, excitement in her eyes. "I'm sure you know from my background check that I was raised in foster care. But what you don't know is how devastating my own learning disability was."

"Then how did you create this program?"

"When I was in school, I didn't have parents who cared to help me with homework," Mia said. "And it wouldn't have been enough anyway. But I had a skill—a superpower, I used to call it. When it came to computers, I had natural ability."

"You must have."

"I struggled to read or write," Mia said. "But I managed to create a simple computer program that helped. Instinct told me that traditional methods had failed me. And I would have failed at life if I hadn't figured things out for myself."

"I must say that I'm impressed."

"I could finally learn," Mia said. "And I've taken that same simple program and expanded it. I've developed it so that it can be used more broadly. Do you understand what that means? Other kids won't have to suffer like I did, won't have to feel like they are idiots because they aren't like other kids. Those kids will have a chance."

Ryker's curiosity was piqued. "You've accomplished all of that when your start in life was the foster system?"

"It was rough," Mia said. "I won't deny that. I've been very public in sharing what happened in my childhood. The abuses were horrific. There are some things the system can't protect a kid from, things that are kept out of the records."

"You were abused?"

Mia's eyes were moist. "I was abused on numerous occasions."

"Were you molested?" Ryker couldn't believe he'd voiced what was on his mind.

"No, I was one of the lucky ones," Mia said. "I know it happens. Heck, it happens in regular families too. Not often, I hope, but I'm not naïve. No, I was battered and unwelcome, except for the support checks I brought in for my 'care.'"

Ryker was deeply moved by what she'd been through, and how she'd dealt with it.

"But I wasn't sexually abused." Mia gave him a devilish grin. "That honor was reserved for my ex-husband."

Ryker fumed inside but held it together. "I'm glad that's over. He won't have that chance again." He furrowed his brow. "What's his problem, anyway?"

"James can't accept the fact that I've divorced him," Mia said. "He's bugged me month after month. Sometimes he's charming, trying to woo me back. And other times he loses it and explodes. He has quite a temper."

"He's too persistent for my liking."

"His efforts to get me back have increased recently," Mia said. "The divorce will be final next month, and that has him backed into a corner. He's become sort of crazed about the whole thing. I've told him repeatedly that there is no chance of reconciliation, but it's like he doesn't hear me."

Ryker thought about that. There was more going on than a jilted lover. The fervor James exhibited was fueled by something more. He had major personality flaws, if he had to harass a woman and stalk her.

He was a threat, maybe just a minor annoyance. Yet Ryker intended to take the matter seriously. Any stalker could appear benign, only to shift into violent behavior. If that happened, Mia wouldn't be alone. Ryker would be there to be sure that no harm came to her.

CHAPTER 5

Mia looked at Ryker, wondering if going to lunch with him had been a good idea. He was irresistible in the cotton shirt that hugged his muscles. She couldn't get the memory of him touching her out of her mind, the way his strong arms had held her tight. Even if it was a self-defense demonstration, it had affected her.

The safer thing would have been to call her driver and go back to work. She could have had lunch brought in as she often did. Yet when Ryker had suggested going out, she'd agreed—despite her better instincts.

She'd wanted to spend lunch with him, and had given in. She needed to reexamine her priorities. It wasn't smart to get involved. There was no reason to think that would happen, anyway. It was a meal together, a chance to get to know her protector.

If she made anything more out of it, that would lead to trouble. Trouble was something that she'd had too much of. The last thing that would be good for her was a pushy male in her life. It was a lesson that had already been learned.

Mia could handle things herself. Although physical safety appeared to be a matter she wasn't as adept at. A history of abuse pointed to the fact it would be a good idea to let Ryker complete her lessons on self-defense.

That was, if she could withstand the attraction.

Ryker looked at her with those blue-gray eyes, making her want to fall into his arms. That didn't mean that was what was going to happen. She had some self-control, after all. But when she looked into those blue depths, she saw sincerity and honesty.

Surely, Mia was deluding herself. There hadn't been a male relationship in her life that had been safe, not when she got to know the man up close and personal. In the beginning, the guy would be on his best behavior, just like Ryker was.

But she was too smart to fall for that. The pretense was shallow and fell apart rapidly, once she grew attached. That wasn't going to happen. Another debacle of a relationship, a controlling influence in her life, might be the end of her.

Mia had forgiven herself for hooking up with James. She hadn't seen through him quickly enough. But she hadn't encountered his personality type before. Abusive types hadn't been scarce, but no one who'd harmed her had been coy about it.

James had been charming, deceiving, and she hadn't spotted the true intent of his pretended affections. Since leaving him, Mia had learned. She'd figured out what she'd done wrong, how she'd missed the signs. Knowing what to look for, she wouldn't botch that again.

Ryker sat across from her, patiently waiting for her to continue.

"Is this your good behavior?" Mia said sharply.

"I'm not sure what you mean."

"Of course you do," Mia said. "This is when you warm me up, get me to cooperate."

"I can protect you better if you do." Ryker frowned. "But I'm not sure what you're driving at. Did I do something to sour your mood?"

"Oh, now it's me. I have a sour mood."

"Listen, I thought we were getting along," Ryker said. "It's helpful for me to understand your background and more about the situation."

"Until I let my defenses down?" Mia felt that happening more with each passing minute.

"You can be a real—"

"Go ahead, say it." Mia pointed her finger at him. "I know what you're going to say. It's good that you are revealing your true self. The care and concern were getting to me, I admit."

Mia hadn't opened up and talked to anyone like she had with Ryker, not in a long time. She shared with her closest friends, but not with a man she'd just met. What had gotten into her?

"Are you trying to start an argument?" Ryker said. "Because if you are, you're doing a damn good job. I was beginning to admire you for all you've accomplished. But I don't get you at all. What are you so afraid of?"

"I'm not afraid, and don't you imply that I am," Mia said. "You don't know anything about me. Just because I told you about my background, don't assume you understand. No one understands, not really."

Mia had done it again. She'd shared something with Ryker that she hadn't intended to. If she didn't know better, she'd think that subconsciously she wanted to get more intimate. But that wasn't going to happen.

"All right," Ryker said. "I don't know you. You've got that part right. I do know one thing: your mood can shift without warning. I'll have to remember that."

Mia was about to spit out the perfect comeback, when an unfamiliar man appeared beside the table. "Excuse me, I'm sorry to interrupt. You're Mia Scott, aren't you? I just want to let you know what a fan I am. I've read about you, and it's an honor to meet you."

Great, there went her privacy. "I appreciate that. Nice to meet you." She should have been more accommodating, but she wasn't in the frame of mind for that. She was tired of being followed everywhere, by one person or the other.

When the man left, Mia said, "Let's get out of here. I'm sure others heard that. I can see it now: our picture on social media. I'm sure we were overheard arguing."

Mia thought of Iris telling her that her picture was on magazine covers. It was too much. It wouldn't help her public image for a post to reveal that she'd been angry with her lunch date. Too much could be made of that, including that she was seeing someone—which she was not.

Once they were outside, Ryker said, "What...are you embarrassed to be seen with me?"

"You just don't get it, do you?"

"Get what?"

Mia didn't want to get into the whole dating implication. She might give Ryker the wrong impression, so she said, "I'm in the public eye. Every move I make is scrutinized, talked about, criticized. I'm running a multimillion-dollar company, and my investors might get nervous."

"All the more reason you should be glad I'm in charge of your protection, instead of fighting me," Ryker said.

"I'll try, but watch it," Mia said. "You got on my bad side with that stunt you pulled of setting up a team to guard me before I'd officially hired you."

"You resent my efforts to keep you safe, and that Caleb scared off trouble before you were seriously injured," Ryker said. "That's what ticked you off? You need to get a grip."

That only made Mia more furious, so she stormed off to the car. "I need to get to the office. *Some* people have work to do."

Ryker opened her door then went around to get in. He glanced over then said, "Why are you looking at your phone like you've just seen a ghost?"

Mia had received a text. She stared at the screen, unable to disguise her chagrin. "Here, look for yourself." She shoved the phone at him.

Ryker read the message out loud: "*I'm annoyed, Mia, that you felt it necessary to hire a bodyguard. I don't know who that guy was who interrupted our conversation, but I'll be back. You'd better warn your muscled companion that if he bullies me, it will only mean harsher actions towards you.*"

"It's a threat," Mia said. "I can't escape that idiot. He won't let me go."

"What does he want?"

"What James wants is for me to go back to him," Mia said, disgusted. "He has his reasons."

"Well, whatever they are, they're not good enough," Ryker said. "He'd better keep his hands off you, or he can bet I'll do more than bully him."

If only it was that simple, but there was so much more to it than that. Mia couldn't get into it with Ryker right then. "I'll deal with him."

"There's something you aren't telling me."

"It's complicated," Mia said. She'd already told Ryker more than she probably should have. Although she wouldn't admit it, deep inside, she liked Ryker and hated to see him get dragged into her messy divorce situation.

Ryker didn't press the issue and drove her to the office. Mia was quiet for the drive, as she'd already made her point. She didn't intend to be charmed and flattered just so the noose could be put around her neck again.

There was no arguing that Ryker was a hunk. And he came from an honorable background as a SEAL. He was in a business that should inspire confidence. But Mia swore that she wouldn't be naïve. If she didn't watch her back, no one else would.

Hiring protection was sensible, but that hadn't put aside her fears about James. She'd dealt with his impulsive and destructive behavior. She'd witnessed his extreme emotional swings—and his explosive anger.

Whatever Ryker thought he was doing to protect her, it likely wasn't enough. James was unpredictable and vicious. She doubted that Ryker had faced such an elusive opponent. He'd fought deadly enemies face to face in battle.

Yet she didn't have confidence that he understood the type of enemy she faced. If she could have explained it, she would have. But she only believed it because she'd lived it. Having experienced abuse, emotional and physical, she knew better than to underestimate James.

When Ryker pulled into the parking lot, Mia said, "You have to understand...James is desperate. He sees the finality of the divorce as a personal threat, for many reasons. Just trust me on that and know that he is a worthy opponent. As much as I despise him, I admit that he's gotten the upper hand far too often. His reference to *harsher actions*...take that warning to heart. He meant it."

Mia left it at that, then went inside to get back to work. She had a full afternoon, with meetings and phone calls. It was exhausting, and she needed a break by the end of the day. Ryker had refused to let Caleb take over. Apparently, he believed what she'd told him, so didn't want to take a chance of anything bad happening to her.

When Mia left the office, Ryker was waiting. "You must be hungry. I'm taking you to dinner."

Mia let out a breath. "Don't you ever *ask*?"

"Apparently, I don't learn quickly," Ryker said. "But you don't scare me. I'm going to look after you, whether you want me to or not."

Mia lifted her hand. "Okay, then. I need a drink. Take me somewhere dark and quiet."

Ryker chose a downtown restaurant, and escorted Mia to the dark interior of the bar. He ordered Coke and she ordered a martini. "You don't drink?"

"Not on the job," Ryker said. "It's better for you if I'm alert."

"True, but I hope you don't mind if I have a drink, maybe two."

"I'm driving," Ryker said, "so have whatever you want."

As much as Mia tried to hold a hard line with Ryker, she found herself talking anyway. He was a good listener, and after a long day, she needed to unwind. He was damn sexy, and the more she spent time with him, the more she felt her defenses crumbling.

It was a pleasure to look at Ryker. He had broad shoulders and a muscled chest. His biceps were bulging at the edge of his sleeves, and his lean thighs were drool-worthy. Mia's mind kept wandering to thoughts she shouldn't have.

As long as Ryker was with her in a public place, she was safe—from him, anyway. Mia really didn't trust herself to be alone with him. She'd made plenty of mistakes in her life, and she didn't want him to be another.

The alcohol went to her head, and she

gradually relaxed. But that didn't mean that Mia had forgotten it wasn't smart to give in to attraction to a controlling male. Drinks and dinner were okay, but no more—definitely not.

Ryker asked more about her company's growth and her software. Mia was willing to talk about safe subjects. She didn't reveal any more than the public knew, or what could easily be found out. But she didn't stop there.

Mia talked about her childhood, about how she survived it, and about her life since she'd been on her own. She talked too much and was aware that she was doing so. But she couldn't seem to stop. Ryker was a good listener, and appeared interested.

"When I was a kid," Mia said, "I didn't have any money, no allowance or anything. So, I went to the public library to use the computer. That's how I got started. I played around, got some ideas, and figured out a way to assist my learning."

"That's clever." Ryker took a gulp of his drink. "When did you own your first computer?"

"Not until I was an adult," Mia said. "My income was barely enough to keep me going before I got into the tech business. I was a theater usher, a waitress…you name it, I did it at some point. When I scraped together a few dollars, I found a used computer at Goodwill."

"I wouldn't have thought of that."

"I took the thing apart and rebuilt it," Mia said. "I had to know how each part worked. I had to see it and touch it with my hands."

"And that helped?"

"For me, it did." Mia drained the last of her cocktail. "I suppose I'm different. I had to be familiar with the inner workings before I could develop software. In my mind, the two were inseparable."

Ryker stared at her, making her feel that maybe he did understand her, just a little.

Mia stood up. "I'm starved. Are you going to feed me or what?" She linked her arm through his, like a real date. It was good to have support. Maybe Ryker was trustworthy. It was a possibility, but she didn't want to assume too much.

Dinner was pleasant, and Ryker even talked a bit. Mia enjoyed hearing about some of the countries he'd been too, and a few anecdotes that he could share without betraying confidentiality. She was curious about his protection business, too.

Ryker filled her in about what type of cases Black Swan handled. But he didn't give many specifics. He told her that protection agents don't reveal any information about their clients. That was good to know. He might be one person that she didn't have to be concerned would violate her privacy.

It was late when Ryker took her home. Mia lived in a nice part of Philly in a condo she'd purchased once her company began doing well. She allowed him to escort her up to her place. Dim lights in the ceiling automatically turned on at dusk, so the main area was illuminated.

Ryker walked into the expansive room. City lights sparkled outside the wall of windows. The white room glowed under the pale cast of the moon. "This is quite a place."

Mia stood next to him and looked out. "I bought it for the view. And I like being up high like this."

"It's easier to keep you safe." Ryker turned to look at her, only a breath away. "The ground floor would present more issues."

The closeness of Ryker's hard body unnerved her. Mia wanted to take a step back yet couldn't manage to do so. She stood so near she could feel his heat and hoped he couldn't read her mind—but maybe he could. When she looked into the depths of his blue eyes, she saw desire.

Ryker's gaze locked with hers, then he touched her cheek. Mia shuddered with need but didn't make a move. "I better go," he whispered, then looked away.

At the door, Ryker said, "The team will work in

shifts. You won't be alone—remember that." Then he went out and shut the door.

*****

For the next few days, Mia tried to push Ryker out of her mind. But it wasn't an easy task. She kept remembering how he looked in the dark bar, the electricity between them at her condo. She wanted to indulge, desired intimacy that she had no right to allow.

And she wanted to trust—only she couldn't.

Mia distracted herself with work, which wasn't difficult. There was plenty to deal with, and long days were required. It was all going to be worth it, then she'd get a break. Maybe next time, she'd be able to enjoy it—with Ryker. But that wasn't going to happen; she was dreaming.

After a stressful afternoon, Iris invited her for drinks with the team. But Mia was exhausted, so she declined. After wrapping things up, she went to the lot and got into her Audi. She really loved that car, and it was good to know that she wouldn't be accosted by her ex again.

Security was around, but Mia got used to that. She saw Caleb frequently, and a few other team members. But they weren't intrusive, so she allowed their presence to blend into the background.

Mia cruised down the street on her way home. It was a pleasant evening, and since she was late, the traffic was light. She cranked up the music and nestled into her leather seat.

A block from Mia's condo, a loud crash startled her, followed by the shattering of the glass in her back window. She shrieked, then looked over her shoulder to see that her trunk was covered with flames. The fire burst into her car, heating the leather and igniting the sleeve of her jacket.

Mia slammed on the brakes, and the Audi skidded over the curb. She patted the flames on her sleeve, putting out the fire that singed her skin. She struggled with her seatbelt. Then the car door opened, and Caleb lifted her out.

Vaguely, Mia saw two others putting out the fire. She leaned against Caleb, fearing for her life. "I've got you," Caleb said. "That was a small firebomb. I saw it and got to you as fast as possible."

Mia glanced back to see burning liquid dripping from her car. Her Audi was trashed; she felt so violated.

"I'll call an ambulance," Caleb said. "Your arm is burned."

"No, please." Mia panicked. "You take me. I'll get there just as fast."

Without argument, Caleb put her in his car. He grabbed a small towel from the backseat then doused it with cool water from a bottle. "Hold this on your skin. I'll get you to emergency as fast as I can."

The pain was bad. It had to be a second-degree burn. Mia was thankful that protection had been nearby. She couldn't imagine how she'd have survived otherwise. She agonized over her physical distress but was more enraged at being a victim. Once again, she'd been a woman alone, an easy target.

Caleb sped her to the hospital, while the rest of the team handled her beloved Audi. There was only one person who could have done this, one person who was jealous and frustrated enough to resort to such tactics. He'd warned her, and he'd made good on his threat.

CHAPTER 6

The night Ryker had escorted Mia to her condo, he'd resisted the urge to kiss her. That wouldn't be right, as he was there to ensure her safety. Indulging in pleasure wasn't on the agenda, as much as he wanted to. Unleashing his desire for a client was unprofessional, as well as dangerous.

If Ryker allowed his emotions to take over, he might make a mistake. He couldn't chance that. He was good at keeping such things buried. Since his wife had died, he'd managed to uphold his duties whether military or civilian.

He'd had to dig deep for the strength to go on, but he was certain that was what Amy wanted. She'd respected him, loved him. He wouldn't let her down. No matter how much he wished for it, he couldn't bring her back. But he could continue to be honorable, to make her proud—and he would.

In the few days since Ryker had seen Mia, she'd been on his mind. It was time to schedule her next self-defense lesson. The only thing was that he feared being close to her would be tempting. One of the other guys could do the training. Only he couldn't bring himself to pass up the opportunity to be with her.

Mia ran hot and cold, but there was something about her that intrigued him. He admired her strength of character. It seemed odd to like a woman for her mind, but he did. She was educated but also street-savvy. Carrying a lipstick taser was an example of her self-reliance, her ability to look out for herself.

Ryker couldn't blame her for resenting the need for protection. She was strong and independent, so he was sure it rubbed her the wrong way. He scrolled to his calendar to look for an open slot for her training. Then his phone vibrated.

The text was all Ryker needed to see; he was out the door and on his way. Caleb's message was that Mia was at the hospital. The thought of her injured sent adrenaline flooding through his veins. Whoever did this would pay.

The drive to the emergency room was a blur. All Ryker could focus on was Mia. He tried not to envision the worst, but it was best to see for himself. Caleb was in the hallway outside the treating room.

"How is she?"

"Mia is going to be fine," Caleb said. "When the doctor is finished treating her burns, she will be able to go home."

Ryker let out a breath. "What the hell happened?"

Caleb relayed the details of the incident. "I saw the bomb toss but there was no time to follow the vehicle. It was more important to rescue Mia. The damn car was on fire."

"Shit, she could have been killed."

"I was behind her, and the other guys were in a second vehicle," Caleb said. "But it took all of us to avoid disaster. The bomb was lobbed at the rear of her vehicle."

"Did you get a look at who did it?"

"The perpetrator was driving an older model Nissan, but it had blacked-out windows," Caleb said. "It all happened so fast, and like I said, it would have been a bad idea to take off after the car."

"Did you get the plate?"

"Couldn't...he sped toward her and threw the bomb on the way by," Caleb said. "He had no front plate."

Ryker was pissed. "Why was Mia driving alone?"

"She refused to have one of us drive her around, said we could follow, but she wasn't going to be chauffeured."

That sounded like Mia. "What kind of injuries?"

"The Audi is totaled," Caleb said, "but Mia scraped by. The doctor is treating a second-degree burn on her right arm."

Ryker raked his hand over his head. "I need to see her. Which room?"

Caleb nodded toward an open door, so Ryker strode down the hall. He pushed open the door to see a nurse tending to Mia.

"I just gave her something for the pain," the nurse said.

Mia looked pale and disheveled, but alive. She had a gauze bandage wrapped around her upper right arm. "Ryker...you got here fast. I just finished with the doctor."

"Are you in much pain? Is there anything I can do?"

"Yeah, it hurts like hell," Mia said. "But Caleb handled the injury at the scene and sped over here. It feels better. The doctor cooled it down then put on antibiotic cream. It will take a bit to heal, but I survived."

Ryker looked at the gauze around her arm and got mad all over again. But he held back from exploding about the asshole who had done this. That could wait, as it would only upset Mia to deal with that now. "How long do you have to stay in here?"

"The doctor should return shortly," Mia said. "He's going to release me with instructions. I don't have to stay overnight, which is good. I don't like hospitals."

"I can't say that I blame you there."

The door opened, and a petite woman with short brown hair ran over to the bed. "Mia, oh my God. I came the instant Caleb called. What an awful thing."

Mia smiled. "I asked him to call you. I didn't know how long I'd be in here, but it looks like I can go home." She looked up. "Ryker, meet my best friend, Iris."

Ryker took her hand and looked into her brown eyes, feeling as though she knew him, even though he hadn't met her before. "My pleasure, Iris."

"Hello, Ryker. I saw you when you came by that first day, but I didn't get a chance to meet you," Iris said. "The pleasure is mine." Her eyes seemed to sparkle.

"Shall I let you ladies talk privately?" Ryker said.

"No, you can stay," Mia said. "Anything we have to say, you can hear."

"I'm horrified that you were injured like this," Iris said. "Things have gotten out of hand."

"I'll have to make a police report, but that can wait until tomorrow," Mia said. "I want to get a grip on the pain. This is the worst burn I've experienced, and it sucks."

"Yeah, no kidding," Iris said, then looked at Ryker. "Where was her protection?"

Mia spoke up. "That's on me. Caleb offered to drive me around, but I wouldn't agree. That was stupid." She sighed. "And now I've lost my Audi."

"I'd be more worried about your skin," Iris said. "You can get another car."

"That's easy for you to say…you know how long I waited to get that Audi."

Iris looked at Ryker. "Can you do anything with her? Because sometimes I can't get her to listen to reason."

Ryker laughed, then glanced at Mia to see if he'd offended her—but she was smiling. "Not so far," he said.

The doctor came in to check on Mia. "That burn should heal up nicely," he said. "It's fortunate your friend brought you in right away. Your arm will hurt for a few days, but you can pick up some painkillers at the drug store. I'll have the nurse give you some supplies to take home. You'll want to keep the wound clean and change the bandage every day."

When the doctor left, Mia said, "I guess that's it. I can go."

"Not so fast, smart girl," Iris said. "Who is going to take care of you?"

Mia said, "I don't need—"

"I am," Ryker said, and both women looked at

him. "I'm going to drive her home and stay with her." He looked at Iris, not willing to listen to Mia's objections. "Are you satisfied?"

Iris grinned. "Yes, very."

Mia slipped out of bed without saying a word to Ryker. "Can you help me change into street clothes, then?" she said to Iris. "I had Caleb go the giftshop and buy something I could wear. My jacket was, uh…burnt to a crisp."

Iris winked at Ryker, then complied with her friend's request. When the women emerged from the bathroom, Mia had on a loose-fitting top that was too big for her. "Let's get you home and more comfortable," Ryker said.

*****

At the condo, Ryker took charge. He didn't care whether Mia liked it or not; he was going to take care of her. But she didn't seem to object. The incident had made an impact on her, as she seemed drawn to him—maybe realizing that he cared about her safety.

Ryker settled Mia in a comfortable chair, then gathered the supplies he'd need. He checked the time, so he'd know when to give her more pills. And he brought her a large glass of water. "You need to stay hydrated. It will help you heal."

"You don't have to do this, you know."

"I want to, so enough said. You can chew me out for something another time," Ryker said. "But

I'm not leaving you alone. Period."

Mia smiled. "I appreciate it. I don't really want to be alone, in pain, and upset. I'm not that masochistic."

Ryker laughed. "Glad to hear it. I was wondering." He put on some music and let her relax. She needed recovery time.

Mia drank her water then asked for a refill. She had her arm propped up, as the doctor had instructed. It would help to keep the burn elevated. She looked at Ryker. "I'm sure you're wondering who did this."

"You know?"

"Not for sure," Mia said. "What's your guess?"

"It could have been an angry fan," Ryker said. "Jealousy knows no limits. Or an investor, blaming you for destabilizing his investment. Shall I go on?"

"It was my ex," Mia said. "It had to be, but I don't have any proof."

Ryker leaned back and put his feet on the coffee table, trying to appear calmer than he was. "Yeah, he was my next guess. What makes you so sure?"

"It just makes sense," Mia said. "He can't get his hands on me, can't release his pent-up anger for defying him. It must be driving him crazy."

"James is that explosive?"

"You don't know the half of it," Mia said.

"Someday I'll fill you in. But my refusal to reunite, or even to talk with him, has pushed him to resort to drastic measures to get my attention."

"He endangered your life."

"That's what's hard to fathom," Mia said. "When he's in a state, he doesn't think of that. He's mad...beyond mad, really. He acts without considering consequences, and he's not thinking about my health and wellbeing."

"I had Jake look into his background, but he couldn't find any dirt," Ryker said.

"James is too clever for that," Mia said. "That's what threw me off for so long. He seems so normal, but rage simmers just below the surface. He wouldn't allow any black marks on his record. He makes sure that the trail doesn't lead back to him. Or if it does, he doesn't look like the guilty one."

Ryker just looked at her.

"I know it sounds bizarre. It took me a while to face up to what I was dealing with."

"A psycho."

"That's one way to put it," Mia said.

Ryker was livid. He'd like to go after the guy, but there was no evidence of wrongdoing—only conjecture. He was beginning to see what Mia was up against. "What about a restraining order?"

"I tried, but it was ineffective," Mia said. "James always figured a way around it—like today's drive-by bombing."

The depth of insanity was alarming. "I'm staying around," Ryker said. "What I mean is that you can't be left alone. There's no telling what that dude will do next. I can't take the chance...*you* can't take the chance."

Mia closed her eyes. "Can you get me a pill? This burn is killing me."

Ryker did as she asked. He kept her as comfortable as possible and waited on her for the rest of the evening. He liked doing so, plus had no intention of leaving her on her own.

It was late, but Mia needed to eat. "What do you feel like having for dinner?"

"I have some leftovers in the fridge," Mia said. "You should find some boxes of Chinese from the other night. I'm sure it's still good. We can share that. And I have ice cream for dessert. I'll come in and help you."

"No, you sit there," Ryker said. "I can take care of it."

Mia patted his arm. "I want to. It will distract me from the pain. I'm not disabled, just injured."

Ryker let her help in the kitchen but kept an eye on her. He was concerned that if she was dizzy or weak, she wouldn't mention it. She tried to be such a tough woman, and she was. But there were occasions when it was okay to have assistance.

Mia seemed fine during dinner. If her arm hurt, she didn't complain. She chatted about other things, anything but her ex-husband terrorizing her. That was best; it would take her mind off the trauma and she'd heal faster.

Dessert was vanilla ice cream with chocolate syrup, which Ryker learned was Mia's favorite. He'd have to remember that. It was a joy to watch her eat it, one spoonful at a time. "Mmm, delicious," she said. "It almost makes me forget that I'm traumatized."

Ryker brushed her hair back from her cheek. "Have as much as you want. I can call Caleb and have him buy more. He can bring it by when he brings my overnight bag."

"You're staying overnight?"

"I thought I made myself clear," Ryker said. "You aren't allowed to be alone. You require protection and nursing. And I'm the best man for the job."

Mia dropped her spoon into the bowl with a clang then smiled. "Bossy."

Ryker took her dishes to the sink. "Get used to it," he said in a lighthearted tone. It was good to see she had a sense of humor.

The condo had two bedrooms, so Ryker took the guest room. He made sure that Mia had everything she needed, then said, "I'll be right here. If you need anything, just yell. I'll leave my door open."

"Okay," Mia said. "And...thanks."

Ryker went to the other room and stripped off his shoes and jeans. He stayed partially dressed, in case he needed to go into action quickly. Although he doubted there was much chance of a break-in. The condo was on the top floor with only one door.

He cleaned up and then stretched out on the bed. It had been a close call, but Mia was safe. He'd have to watch her more closely. He'd underestimated her ex-husband's vindictiveness, but he was up to speed now, and didn't intend to let the guy gain any advantage.

Mia had struggled with stuff like this on her own for years, for her entire life, really—if he considered that she'd been raised in foster homes. She was an amazing woman who had come close to falling through the cracks in society.

There were no provisions for young girls without parents who couldn't learn like other students. It must have been rough. Ryker wanted to hold Mia in his arms, to tell her how much he respected her. And to tell her more than that.

He didn't know what he'd tell her. But deep emotions bubbled up from below the surface. If he didn't watch it, he'd feel much more for Mia than he should. He needed to stay focused on her protection. It had been a while since he'd considered sharing his life with a woman.

And he couldn't believe that he'd thought of doing so with Mia. She was a woman he could love, whom he could care for. But it wasn't going to work. His heart was permanently broken, and had shown no signs of healing, in all these years.

Plus, Mia was an independent woman. She wasn't looking for a man to hook up with. Just the opposite—she was trying to get away from the last one. Under the circumstances, it was best to go to sleep and forget about her—but his heart ached.

*****

At breakfast, Mia was cheerful. She'd been able to shower and dress on her own. "I wrapped my arm in plastic. And the pain is less."

"That is good news." The doorbell rang, so Ryker went to answer it. He was expecting Caleb, who handed him a duffel bag and a sack of groceries.

"You good in there?" Caleb said.

"Yep, Mia is recovering. Text if you need me. I'm going to stay close to her for now."

Ryker returned and unloaded the groceries. "I got some supplies for us. And a change of clothes."

Mia's eyes widened. "More ice cream? You're going to fatten me up."

"We'll see about that." Ryker watched her scramble some eggs. "I thought I was taking care of you."

"And you do it well," Mia said. "But I'm not an invalid. I tend to get into trouble, I admit. But I'm able to whip up some eggs and toast."

Over the meal, Ryker pried more details out of Mia about her ex. He needed to know all he could about his adversary. He had to get the upper hand, so the more he knew, the better.

Mia drank the rest of her orange juice. "I screwed up marrying James, but I did one thing right. We didn't have children. I was convinced that we should be together for a year or so before taking on that responsibility."

"It is good that no kids are involved."

"James is greedy and self-important," Mia said. "He would have been a lousy father."

Ryker drank his coffee and listened.

"Looking back, I'm sure that James was interested in my company," Mia said. "My start-up was just beginning to take off, so my attorney advised me to have him sign a prenuptial agreement."

"I bet that went over well."

"James didn't like it, but there wasn't much he could do about it," Mia said. "He was being charming and didn't want to blow it. Of course, I didn't see that then. The only way he can tap into the financial success of my company now is through marriage. If he could wheedle his way back into my life, he'd take control."

Mia continued, "But once this divorce is final, he's out of luck. He can't face that. He wants to take it all, and he would have, if I hadn't come to my senses."

"No wonder he's so bent out of shape," Ryker said. "And I imagine it's a blow to his ego, as well. I'm beginning to catch on, see what kind of person he is."

"That's a good way to put it," Mia said. "James will see losing me as a failure."

Ryker took her hand, and she squeezed it. "I am glad you're with me right now. This is a rough period." Then Mia looked into his eyes. "What about you? I don't see a ring on your finger. Have you ever been married?"

Ryker's gut twisted. The guilt was powerful. "I was married, but my wife Amy died."

Mia was quiet.

"I met her after I joined the Navy, and we married," Ryker said. "She was the love of my life, and I missed her so much when I was away. We never had kids either. We were married for five years and planned to have a family when I got out."

Ryker looked into Mia's eyes, finding empathy but not pity. "Amy died while I was on deployment. I wasn't here. I should have been with her."

"How did she die?"

"My wife was hit by a drunk driver. She was killed on impact," Ryker said. "And I didn't even get the satisfaction of making the bastard pay for his crime. His car went over an embankment, so he didn't survive the crash either."

"Ryker...that must be so hard for you."

Mia had no idea the magnitude of the sadness that consumed him. Every day since his wife had died, Ryker had agonized about what he could have done to prevent it, or how he should have been home. But none of it mattered. The past couldn't be changed. He had to live with it.

CHAPTER 7

That night in bed, Mia thought about Ryker. He'd been so good to her. It had been the first time a man had taken care of her, and it took some getting used to. With her arm propped up on pillows, she was almost able to fall asleep, but not right away.

It hadn't escaped her notice how much enjoyment Ryker got from watching her eat ice cream. He was going to buy gallons of the stuff at this rate. Mia tried to comprehend that his pleasure was because of hers. That was something new.

With her husband, it had all been fake. James had smiled and cajoled, but he'd quickly shifted from the loving persona to the self-centered man he truly was. Mia should be on guard, and she was, but Ryker was different.

Mia could tell that his attitude was authentic. She'd learned about clues to deception, and he didn't exhibit those. He was a study in a good-hearted, honest man. She hadn't known that such a male existed, at least not for her.

She'd met men, even Griffen, her manager,

whom she trusted. But not personally, not enough to have an intimate relationship. Dating was fine, but other than James, she hadn't bonded with any man or wanted anything more—until she met Ryker.

He had gotten under her skin and was working his way into her heart. That thought was frightening. She was used to threats and attacks, so had learned how to fight back. But she had no defense against Ryker's kindness. She closed her eyes to block him out of her mind, but the feeling in her heart didn't go away.

For the moment, Mia was safe, but how long would that last? She had protection, yet it might not be enough. James was acting like a madman, which was an appropriate description. She remembered how he'd treated her, how shocked she'd been when he'd given in to his temper.

James had tried to put that on her, claimed that she caused him to react that way. What was amazing was that she believed it at first, so attempted to alter her behavior. But it had been a lie. It hadn't taken long for her to see that he was manipulating her.

Just like he wanted to do now.

If he could bully or scare her into cooperating with him, then he would win. Yet he hadn't realized that wasn't going to happen. She was over him for good, saw him for the man he was.

All she wanted to do was get away—with her company and her life.

*****

For the next few days, Ryker stayed close. He catered to her needs, despite the fact that she knew he had better things to do—and told him so. He claimed he didn't, that taking care of her was the most important thing. After a while, she began to believe that he meant it.

Ryker drove her to the office as soon as she was able to return. Mia couldn't argue, since she didn't have her car yet. She'd need to buy another one, but the insurance hadn't come through. It didn't matter so much, since she felt better being escorted.

It had been bad timing to be away from her company. Fortunately, Griffen and Iris had kept things going. But there were some items on the agenda that only Mia could handle. She spoke with edgy investors regarding their investments.

The distribution progress wasn't fast enough, and confidence had waned. The news about Mia being held at gunpoint and robbed, followed by being injured from a car bomb, only worsened sentiment. She did her best to restore faith in Mental Magic and its new learning program.

Griffen caught her up on recent events. "The Board of Education is balking," he said. "A meeting needs to be set up. If that stalls, we'll have serious issues."

"I'll arrange something," Mia said. Her life had been a series of disasters. Yet she'd done one right thing by creating the software. The technique used in the program had been the one that had saved her, allowed her to learn in a new way—and it would save others. It could be the hope for children with issues like she'd had.

There was big money on the line, and Mia couldn't fail. She called a meeting with her staff to remind them of their greater purpose. The reason investors had backed the company was due to the carefully prepared business plan. The idea was to start locally, then expand, eventually distributing internationally. The potential was exciting, but only if they made it through this crucial period.

It was important to think big and to profit fast. Delays could drag the company under. Mia assured her team that she had no intention of letting that happen. She looked over at Griffen, who nodded at her. She had to make her words true; she had to ratchet up the effort and get the job done.

It was early afternoon before Iris came to her office. "I'm starving. All these negotiations and pep talks are wearing me out. Come on, let's go eat."

Mia could certainly use lunch. The coffee and eggs she'd had for breakfast weren't enough. "We can eat at the café around the block. And don't be surprised, but I have transportation for us."

Iris widened her eyes. "A hunky SEAL?"

"Yep, this time it's Caleb, because Ryker had some matters to attend to."

"Other than you?" Iris said. "I'm shocked."

Mia playfully punched her shoulder. "Oh, come on. I know what you're thinking. You're making way too much of Ryker playing nurse to me."

When Mia got to the parking lot, Caleb was ready. To his credit, he didn't give her a hard time about not accepting his rides before. That was just as well, since she'd learned how important protection could be. Until James went away, she'd err on the side of caution.

Over lunch, Mia talked to Iris about her messy divorce. "These past years have been a nightmare."

"And it's crunch time," Iris said. "If James has any tricks he hasn't used, he'll try them now. He's nearly out of time."

"I'm glad you understand," Mia said. "It would make more sense for him to try to sweet-talk me. But that's not James. What drives him only he understands, because I don't. I stopped trying to figure him out long ago."

"Your experience makes me glad that I'm single," Iris said, then took a sip of her iced tea. "I wish they'd hurry up with those sandwiches. A woman could starve to death."

As if the waiter had overheard, he appeared with the meals. Iris lifted half of her turkey sandwich and took a big bite. "I might survive the afternoon."

Mia thought of Ryker and the grilled cheese sandwiches he'd made the day before. Why was it that everything was a reminder of him? Then her phone vibrated, and she hoped that he was checking on her.

But it was James calling. "I'm going to take this," Mia said. "I have to give this bastard a piece of my mind." She went outside to take the call.

"You have a lot of nerve," Mia said. "Just what do you think you're doing?"

"I don't know what you mean," James said. "I'm calling to try and talk to you...again."

"How can I make myself any clearer? I don't want to talk to you about *anything*." Mia grimaced when a pain shot through her arm. "And you hurt me, you creep."

"I don't know what you mean," James said. "I'm trying to fix things between us."

Always the liar, the pretender. Mia couldn't take it. "It isn't going to happen. Just leave me alone. You scare me."

"You should be scared," James said, "because if you aren't nicer to me, I'll have to do something

I'd rather not do. But you appear to be forcing me into it."

That line again; *she* was always the one making James behave the way he did. Mia was about to hang up. Speaking with her ex had been a bad idea.

"The Board of Education is considering your proposal for implementation," James said.

Mia gripped the phone.

"With all that's been happening to you lately, it's difficult for the board to have confidence," James said. "I might have to affirm their doubts and tell them exactly why they shouldn't do business with you."

"That is just wrong."

"Oh, is it?" James said. "What's *wrong* is you divorcing me. Till death do us part, remember?"

And there it was: Mia's biggest mistake. James was on the board and held an executive position. He was respected, and his coworkers paid heed to his opinions. It seemed they weren't aware of his true nature. He was an upstanding citizen, a man of character.

"Don't do it," Mia said. "Think of those children, the ones who need the program. It's about learning, about education, about giving them a chance. Don't let your feelings about me take away their ability to learn, an opportunity for a decent future."

"It didn't help you any," James said. "You should be glad that I take an interest in you, that I married you. It's more than you deserve."

Mia put her hands over her eyes. James was seething; she could hear it in his voice.

"You're an orphan," James said. "You had no place in life until you met me, and I took you on out of the goodness of my heart. Don't talk to me about your precious software. It didn't help you. You're still the same stupid bitch that begged me to marry her."

Tears poured down Mia's cheeks. The call ended. She was too choked up to speak anyway. It wasn't because James had demeaned her. She was used to that. It was because she saw the chance to help so many young students slip away. Failure loomed, and it broke her heart.

Mia wiped away the tears. She was furious. James had reminded her why she didn't want to hook up with any man. He'd shattered her trust and got perverse pleasure from stomping on her self-esteem. No more bad experiences. It had to end.

She went inside to find Iris finishing her meal. "Oh, God...what did he say?"

"He's just...insane," Mia said. "I don't know how far he will go to stop me."

Iris glanced toward the front of the restaurant. "Caleb is hovering by the door. He must have seen you talking. James is going to have a difficult time getting to you with all that muscle behind you."

"He doesn't need to get his hands on me," Mia said, then shared what the conversation had been about.

"He wouldn't?"

"Yes, he will, so we have to contact our friends on the board," Mia said. "Somehow we have to make them see what he's doing."

"Which reminds me, aren't we going to the school this afternoon?"

"Yes, I hadn't forgotten." Mia had supported after-school programs, even visited students once a month to help.

Lunch was over, so Mia let Caleb know where to drive them next. She looked forward to interacting with the elementary school students, especially one young boy.

Eddie was eight years old. He was small for his age but very bright. He was clever and funny. Mia adored him and opened her arms for a hug when she spotted him. "It's good to see you."

"Are we going to play games?" Eddie had big brown eyes and curly brown hair. She'd known him since before he'd entered school. The boy had trouble learning, and he had another strike against him: James was his uncle.

James didn't care about his sister's only son. But it was worse than that. He was embarrassed by him, couldn't stand it that the child needed help—as if that somehow was a bad reflection on James. He'd abandon his own flesh and blood, rather than be associated with a boy who had a learning disability.

"Yes, we are going to play," Mia said. "And I have a new game for you."

Eddie's eyes shone. "Hey, Iris. Are you going to be there too?"

"You bet I am." Iris took his hand to lead him to the classroom. "I have a few things to learn, too, so I'll join you."

Mia had learning tools on a disc that she'd brought with her. She couldn't officially distribute her software, but she could use it. The methods aided Eddie, and it was rewarding to see him discover that he wasn't stupid as he'd so often been told.

The key to the games, as Eddie called them, was that they were more visual. Visual learners had trouble with written words. Her tool used a wide array of colors and set up codes the child could more easily remember. It was a method that made sense to Eddie, as opposed to him struggling to learn the standard way.

At the end of the day, Mia and Iris met the team for drinks and dinner. Everyone had been working hard, so deserved a break. Griffen made a toast to the team, stating with pride about how they were together in this and would come through. Nothing worthwhile was achieved without struggle.

Mia drank and smiled and encouraged her staff. Yet she knew there was a difficult fight ahead. She vowed to lead her team to success. She couldn't let James get in her way. He wasn't in control anymore, not in her business or her life.

CHAPTER 8

Mia wasn't far from Ryker's thoughts. He'd arranged for Caleb and his crew to stay close and watch for any signs of trouble. There had been a phone call that had appeared to upset Mia, so he planned to ask about that.

Meanwhile, Ryker had been at headquarters tending to business. As the cofounder, he had a vested interest in the company. Black Swan was expanding at a rapid rate, as there was an increasing demand for executive protection.

That was good for business but had been keeping Ryker away from Mia. He'd called to invite her to dinner. It was time to catch up and find out what the phone call that day had been about.

Ryker continued to stay in Mia's guestroom at night, but she'd been very busy and appeared stressed. He didn't bug her by asking; she'd tell him when she was ready. It didn't pay to interfere, but that didn't mean that he wouldn't keep a close eye on her.

The bickering between them was at a

minimum, partially because of so few chances to talk. That's another thing Ryker could remedy at dinner. The truth was that he looked forward to seeing Mia. She was a special woman, and he couldn't deny that he was drawn to her.

One advantage to getting immersed in his duties was that it allowed for separation from her. As much as Ryker liked being around Mia, he dared not take that too far. He had his boundaries and intended to stick to them.

Letting his heart get involved would only lead to trouble. He'd had love in his life once and lost it. He saw no reason to chance that again. Yet he desired Mia. He just couldn't let her know that, so he'd been on his best, most professional behavior.

It was his job to protect Mia, so that was where Ryker needed to focus. He cared enough about her to put her safety first. And he was duty-bound, something he didn't take lightly. His responsibilities came first, putting his personal feelings in second place—although not as remote as he would have liked.

Ryker left early to go home and change clothes. He dressed comfortably, yet appropriate for a dinner date. It mattered what Mia thought, which was also something new. He rarely cared about such things. On the way downtown to pick her up, he looked forward to seeing her.

*****

Ryker waited for Mia at reception, but it wasn't long before she came out. On one side, her stylish hair was swept up into a gold clip. She wore a cream-colored jacket with flowing slacks that looked more like a skirt than pants.

Whatever Mia wore seemed to suit her. She had a knack for choosing smart casual wear, an ambiguous description for the polished yet relaxed way she dressed. Ryker imagined that she had a lot of practice putting together outfits.

Mia hadn't needed to go home to change for dinner, because she looked as designer-perfect at her office as she did privately. Or maybe it was just that Ryker was enamored with her. How she presented herself, her demeanor, her confidence—all of it was attractive.

"You look nice," Ryker said, keeping his reaction subdued.

Mia smiled. "That's kind of you."

Ryker looked at reception to find Iris watching. "Make sure she gets some downtime. Mia has been overworking. Don't let her cool, calm attitude fake you out."

Mia grinned. "Never mind Iris. She's been working as much as I have."

Ryker escorted Mia to the car, paying attention to what was around them. He didn't pick up any indication of danger, but that didn't prevent him from staying alert. He was on duty, as pleasurable an assignment as that might be.

During the drive, Mia talked about the last couple of days, without mentioning any upsetting phone call. It looked like Ryker would have to bring it up. He'd wait until she'd had a drink, hoping she'd be more willing to open up to him about any distress.

She tried to be so tough, making Ryker want to shoulder some of the burden, if she'd let him. The restaurant had an outdoor patio, which would be a good place to chill out. Mia would get that downtime Iris had mentioned.

Ryker followed her to a table in the garden setting. He tried to quell his attraction, but it was useless. Mia was a gorgeous, brilliant, caring woman. His admiration for her grew by the day. He was on dangerous ground and he knew it.

The restaurant used local ingredients and had a list of unique signature cocktails. Mia sat across from him on the open-air veranda, appearing pleased with his choice to eat there. She glanced over at the greenery that surrounded the patio. "What a lovely garden. This is a great place to escape from the bustle of Center City. I'll have to remember to come here again."

The place was crowded and noisy, filled with business types who worked nearby. It seemed to be an after-work hangout. "What will you have?" Ryker said.

"I think I'll have a mimosa. I know those are Sunday brunch fare, but I rarely go out then."

Once the orders were placed, Mia said, "You're having a beer?"

"I thought I would. It's a low-alcohol one, not likely to put me out of commission."

"It better not. You're my guard for the evening. Caleb will get on your case if you screw up."

It was good to see that Mia was acclimating to having a security detail. He liked it when she was playful, so much more than when she was in a challenging frame of mind. He could handle verbal fencing with the best of them, but he preferred to enjoy an amiable evening.

The drinks arrived, and Ryker leaned back with his beer, content to look at Mia. She talked for a bit, about nothing in particular. He found he could listen to her for hours on end, although he hadn't had the chance to put that to the test.

When Mia was halfway through her drink, Ryker took the plunge. "I need to ask you a question. Was there a phone call that upset you?"

"Caleb can't keep a secret, can he?" Mia said, then proceeded to tell him about her conversation with James. Surprisingly, she didn't seem reluctant to relay what had happened. "Not only did he refuse to confess that he'd firebombed my car, he threatened me. He will counter my efforts with the Board of Education."

"If physical violence won't gain your compliance then he's not above using other tactics."

"I think you're catching on," Mia said. "James is cruel and doesn't value my emotional health anymore than my physical safety. He wants me to obey, so he's blind to all else."

Ryker ordered a drink refill for Mia and a Coke for himself. She seemed thoughtful.

"Is there something on your mind?"

"We talk about me a lot of the time," Mia said. "I hope you don't mind me asking, but I'd like to know more about your wife—if you're okay with talking about it."

"I can tell you more about Amy." Ryker swallowed hard, affected by grief, even so many years after her death. "But if you want to know how I dealt with the loss...I haven't. It weighs heavily on my conscience, and I miss her. I suppose that I always will."

Ryker proceeded to tell Mia about his wife, including how he'd met her at a holiday party. She was a friend of a friend, and he'd liked her from the start. She was warm and sincere, a lovely person. After knowing her for six months, he'd come home on leave and married her.

"It's been more than ten years since her death," Ryker said. "It seems...so long ago. She will always have a place in my heart, but I try not to dwell on what could have been."

Mia listened without comment.

Ryker wasn't in the habit of talking about his wife's death, yet he had been okay with sharing some of it with Mia. It occurred to him that in all the years since, Mia was his first close relationship with a woman.

He wasn't certain that he could move past the loss, but it felt good to tell Mia. For some reason, he wanted her to know about his first love, and sensed that she understood. The meals arrived, interrupting their discussion.

Even while talking, Ryker hadn't abandoned his protection duties. He'd kept an eye on his surroundings, on the patio and beyond. Waitstaff cruised in and out of the main restaurant but exhibited no unusual behavior.

The patrons on the patio filled all the tables, engaged in their own conversations. Ryker observed the others yet didn't find anyone who appeared out of place. There had been no attention directed at Mia, so the restaurant hadn't posed any threat.

Then a small light flickered from the sidewalk, probably a camera flash from a distance. The shrubbery along the walkway rustled, but no person was visible. The signs of surveillance alerted Ryker. The activity outside the restaurant had caught his attention. And there was a van across the street that had arrived shortly before.

He noted the name of the company, so he could check on its validity.

Dinner was almost over. Ryker hesitated to alarm Mia, but he had to let her know. "Don't look around, but I think we're being watched."

Mia's eyes widened. "What makes you think so?"

Ryker told her what he'd observed. "The best thing to do is for us to behave normally. Act like you don't know you've been observed. I'd rather keep whoever is watching off guard."

It was best to get Mia to the car, then home safely. They'd skip dessert at the restaurant, plus there was plenty of ice cream at home. Without revealing any alarm, Mia went to the car with him. Ryker looked ahead for any danger and stayed close to her. If he needed to block an attack, he'd be in an advantageous position.

Once Mia was safely in the car, Ryker got into the driver's side then locked the doors. The vehicle's bulletproof windows gave him some piece of mind, but he was intent on getting back to the condo without delay. Until he found out who was behind this, he couldn't relax.

*****

The next day, Caleb and the team implemented additional strategies for Mia's safety, while Ryker took steps to uncover what was behind the incident. It could have been a curious fan, but he couldn't dismiss threats quite so fast.

Hawke agreed that the matter should be taken seriously. "The first step is to discover who is watching Mia. Then we can follow that up and see where it leads."

"My suspicion is that James is behind this," Ryker said. "He is the most likely one, so let's watch him more closely. I'd like to see what he's up to."

Right after the bomb incident, surveillance had been set up on James. Watching was ongoing from two vantage points. The first was surveillance on his home, plus monitoring his digital communications, as much as Jake was able to.

The second observation point was from protection agents who blended in with his normal activities. Whether he was going to lunch or stopping at the drugstore, agents traded off following him. That way it wasn't the same men, making it difficult to spot—not that James was savvy about such clandestine activities.

Ryker spoke with Jake. "I need to know about his contacts, any phone calls, emails...anything that would shed light on his activities at present."

A more in-depth workup would be done on James, meant to uncover his strategy before he was able to implement any damaging plan. Before that was achieved, Ryker learned that the camera flash he'd spotted was someone photographing

Mia eating dinner with him.

The pictures made a splash across social media then went viral before Ryker could blink an eye. It was Ryker having dinner with a client, but the posts announced that he was dating her. The *new man in her life* was a repeating theme in numerous threads.

That night, Ryker tried to reassure Mia, to no avail.

"Are you kidding me?" Mia said. "It's an invasion of privacy. I don't care if I was dating you…which I am not. It's nobody's business."

Ryker stared at the images on his phone. It did look romantic. He'd been deep in conversation, and Mia's expression was emotional. The photos of the intimate discussion gave the wrong impression. He hadn't spotted the cameraman soon enough.

"I know it was James," Mia said, anger flashing in her eyes. "It had to be."

"I'm assuming he hired an investigator to follow you around," Ryker said. "I expect confirmation on that from Jake."

"My ex-husband has the nerve to employ a PI so he can keep tabs on every move I make." Mia expelled a breath.

"With that important board meeting only days away, I imagine he wants any ammunition he can get."

"Well, I certainly gave him some," Mia said. "But it's not a crime to date. The divorce is final in a month. Even if I was going out with you, what's the big deal?"

"You're a celebrity, as far as your supporters are concerned," Ryker said. "Snooping into your private life is common practice, so I'm not surprised the pictures went viral."

"What does James hope to gain by that?"

That question was promptly answered, as the aggravating situation took a turn for the worse.

"Take a look at this," Ryker said, handing his phone over.

"Oh my God. He wouldn't! He can't." But he had.

James had posted that he was shocked and hurt by Mia's behavior. That wouldn't have been so bad. But he'd posted more photographs that he claimed had fallen into his hands.

"Those are fake," Mia said. "That just didn't happen."

The pictures were of Ryker and Mia, showing them doing various things together that they hadn't done. It took nerve to perpetrate such lies. The altered photos wouldn't go undetected. Photoshopped images would be obvious to a trained eye.

"I know this is all a lie...and you know it," Ryker said. "The problem is that proving the photos are fake may not resolve the issue. The outcome depends less on that, and more on what the public wants to believe."

"It's more scandal to go with what James has alleged," Mia said. "I fear that denying it will only make it worse."

If one was to believe what James had posted, then Mia had been seeing Ryker for quite a while. In fact, Ryker was responsible for breaking up her marriage. He was maligned for his role as protector, because he was the one Mia needed protection from.

It was a nightmare. The attempt to trash Mia's reputation had pulled Ryker into the mess. He hadn't been careful enough; he'd given the enemy opportunity, and James had taken it. It would be assumed that Mia was untrustworthy and had betrayed her husband's faith in her.

Even in an age where divorce was not uncommon, the public was quick to point a finger at a celebrity or public figure for moral transgressions. What was presented for public examination rarely held up well.

"It will make it worse if you try to explain," Ryker said. "Any defense will only look like an admission of guilt."

It was amazing how fast news travelled via social media. It seemed that no sooner had James posted his vile allegations than others jumped into the controversy. Questions abounded about how Mia met Ryker, why was he in charge of her security, was he after Mia's money, and the list went on.

At every turn, James embellished the false claims, creating more questions and more doubt. His backstabbing approach to make Mia buckle to his will had created havoc in the span of hours.

"Do you realize what all of this will sound like to the Board of Education?" Mia said. "They don't live in a cave. The members read this stuff. And don't think that James won't use it to his best advantage. He will attend that meeting and pretend innocence. He'll play the part of the injured husband, abandoned by his wife after a year...his *adulterous* wife."

Mia flopped onto the sofa then covered her eyes. "I hate him. I really do."

"He will make a mistake," Ryker said. "He's making bold moves, taking risks."

Mia looked at him. "You don't know James like I do...what he's gotten away with, how clever he can be. He can turn anything to his advantage. I've seen him do it, over and over."

Ryker had no doubt of the truth of her statement. One thing was certain: he was going to attend the board meeting with Mia. He'd do all he could to protect her, yet he'd discovered that physical protection wasn't all there was to ensuring her safety.

CHAPTER 9

One morning, Mia met Iris for coffee. She needed to vent, as things had gotten out of control. The trendy café was close to the office, had good coffee, and even roasted the beans on site. The décor was gray and white, with flowered wallpaper and marble counters.

The place was one of Mia's favorites. She sat at a wooden table, sipping her latte and chatting. Iris was a good listener, and she offered valuable input. With everything going on, it was a high-voltage situation. Security wasn't far—that day, Caleb and his guys had the shift.

"All the news about you lately has caused quite a sensation," Iris said.

"It doesn't seem to stop." Mia sighed. "No sooner than I recover from one drama, something else happens."

"And James is flat-out lying."

"What else is new?" Mia said. "That's him. He can lie like no one else I've known. I wish I hadn't met him."

"But adultery...really?" Iris rolled her eyes. "That's something *he's* capable of. In fact, I'd be more inclined to believe he was talking about himself than about you."

"Oh, please," Mia said. "He wouldn't admit any wrongdoing; it was always me."

"How did Ryker take it?"

"He took it in stride," Mia said. "What else could he do? And he tried to calm me down, but it's my life we're talking about. I won't be pushed around. I refuse to permit it."

"James is transgressing boundaries. If he doesn't watch it—"

"No, he's too clever," Mia said. "That's what's so aggravating. He gets away with this stuff."

"How is it going with Ryker?"

Mia took a sip of her drink, thinking that over. "You mean that he's staying at the condo? I feel safer, under the circumstances. But you're my best friend, so I can tell you...he is a very attractive man."

Iris laughed. "That's an understatement. The guy is a total hunk, and you know it. Plus, he's sleeping in the bedroom next to you every night."

"You don't have to tell me," Mia said. Each night, she thought of Ryker so close. The electricity between them couldn't be denied, but that didn't make getting intimate a good idea. "I'm resisting. That's all I need is a messy relationship, while all this other stuff is going on."

Mia needed to focus on the business at hand,

which was keeping her company profitable. And the meeting with the advisory group for the board was very soon.

*****

The morning of the meeting, Mia changed clothes three times. She couldn't make up her mind what to wear. She ended up calling Iris. "Should I go with a suit, look formal and all-business? Or is casual better?"

"Be yourself," Iris said. "The members want to meet you and, to a degree, will base their decision on whether you connect with them. That's how it works these days."

That was sage advice, but Mia wasn't sure what being herself meant anymore. With so much change, it was difficult to gain firm footing. It seemed that one day she'd been a struggling student, and the next she was expected to manage a high-profile company.

Some days, it was too much. Mia thought about what was at stake; that was what kept her going. Eddie and other children were unaware of the pressures of her career. Yet they depended on her to come through for them.

Ryker cooked breakfast, but Mia was too nervous to eat. "I'll just have coffee." *He* looked yummy enough to eat in his polo shirt and slacks. But she couldn't afford any distractions.

"You look nice."

"You think this will work?" Mia had chosen a satin blouse and matching pants in a soft fabric. "I'm hoping to look professional, yet approachable."

Ryker handed her a cup of coffee. "I don't understand all the nuances of how to dress to impress. But I'm sure the members will admire your choice of outfit."

"That's not the point," Mia said. "This meeting is a big deal. It's not with the Board of Education, as that organization doesn't meet directly. There is an advisory group of parents and community members. What the group recommends carries a lot of weight."

Ryker sat across from her. "I suppose that makes sense. It's a way for the officials to understand what's wanted in the educational system."

"I have to make them see the advantages of my product," Mia said. "But James will be there. He's on the board and volunteered to represent them." That was what she dreaded most.

After dumping the dishes in the sink, Ryker drove her to the meeting. He wouldn't allow anyone else to take over security on such an important day. He'd told her that he wanted to be there for moral support. On the way, Mia rehearsed what she'd say for the hundredth time. She was a bundle of nerves.

When Mia arrived, it was good to see that Griffen and Iris were already there. At least she didn't have to do this alone. The room was like most school meeting rooms, with a long Formica table and aluminum chairs with beige plastic seats. The walls were dirty white, and the floor was linoleum.

For a moment, Mia was back in school. All her young years she'd felt trapped by the dull atmosphere of the educational system, the struggle to learn. She understood what students endured, and remembering that fueled her purpose to do something about it.

Gradually, the members of the advisory board filtered in. Mia noticed that each member looked at her, as if deciding whether she was acceptable. In general, the members were parents concerned for their children's education. She hoped to demonstrate the value of what she had to offer.

The overall tone was conservative, which was expected in such a forum. Mia could work with that; she'd become skilled at presenting from all the interactions with investors. Speaking to a group of parents shouldn't be so bad.

And it wouldn't have been, except for the one person whose arrival she dreaded.

A middle-aged woman wearing tortoiseshell glasses ran the proceedings. Her name was Sarah, and she gave a short rundown of her duties. Mia introduced herself, along with Griffen and Iris, letting the group know their roles and that they were the core of her team.

Ryker stood by the door, looking very former military. He received a scrutinizing look.

"This is Ryker Johnson from Black Swan Protection. He will be observing." Mia smiled at the group. "It is part of the corporate world to have executive protection." She didn't mention any of the recent news stories about her and was relieved that no questions about that were asked.

Mia had brought a slide presentation, so she set that up with Griffen's assistance, while Iris interacted with a few of the members. So far, the group seemed amenable to hearing what Mental Magic was about and what the software could do for students with learning difficulties.

Detailing the software and its use would be the central part of the presentation. Mia was proficient with that, since she'd done it so many times to gain financial support. In many ways, this event would be so much easier. It was more low-key than making her case to potential investors asking pointed questions to judge whether to risk their money.

James arrived late, which was likely intentional. It was his habit to orchestrate personal interactions, so he was the center of attention. When he entered the room, all eyes were on him. He looked cool as a cucumber as he strolled over to the table.

He wore a tailored charcoal suit with a light blue shirt, making Mia wish that she'd opted for a business suit instead of her casual outfit. His thick hair was nicely groomed, his close beard shaved to perfection. Turning on the charm, he went to Sarah, greeting her as though she was a close friend.

With a practiced smile, James held her hand sandwiched between his, exuding warmth. Sarah blushed then turned to the group to introduce him. Most of the members seemed to know him, or at least knew who he was, since he was on the board.

Mia's thoughts flashed to a movie she'd seen years before about Ted Bundy. All who'd known him had described him as a charming man. He'd been a volunteer at a suicide hotline and a college graduate. It seemed that not one person saw through his façade or suspected that he was serial killer. She'd marveled at how a psycho could hide his true nature from the outside world.

Watching James in action wasn't so different. Mia blinked and looked away; she was freaking herself out. Her ex-husband wasn't a murderer...surely. He was a manipulator, able to turn sentiment to his favor with seeming ease. She made a note to be cautious of him, as he was in rare form at the meeting.

In no hurry, James went around the table, shaking hands with each attendee. He was buttering them up, but that didn't seem apparent to anyone but Mia. She shuddered to think about all the times he'd done something similar. It hadn't led to anything good.

With a flourish, James took a seat at last. Only then did he acknowledge the presence of Mia and her team. The intentional slight was for effect; he clearly hoped to put her at a disadvantage from the start. "Mia," he said with a cursory nod.

It didn't go unnoticed that he addressed her by first name only, even though she was the presenter. It demonstrated a lack of respect. He glanced at her team members but offered no greeting. And he completely ignored Ryker, as if her protection didn't exist.

Mia's stomach was in a knot. She rose from her chair and began the presentation, pretending that James wasn't glaring at her. She went through the slides, speaking clearly and with confidence. She went over the schedule for the distribution of the learning tool into schools.

The concept was to provide a summer program for the youth in need, before testing in the fall. For some of the students, it would be a last chance before being held back again. She stressed the need for important learning outcomes, such as giving a child a strong sense of identity and making them feel connected, able to contribute to the world around them.

She shared her personal story, telling what it had been like for her in similar circumstances, yet how she'd managed to develop a tool that turned things around for her. The concept of her company was to implement that very tool, only greatly refined and improved, into the school system.

Then she talked about students she interacted with, ones she'd personally worked with in testing the program. She didn't want to talk about a vague student body, faceless and nameless. She spoke of Eddie and the gains that he'd made, without chancing a glance at James, already knowing she'd find a look of disdain.

She ended with a plea for the committee's support and voiced her concern for other children like Eddie. It would be heartless to deny those students the assistance that was available. Then she smiled at the group and took her seat.

She glanced at Ryker, who watched with a look of pride. It felt good to have him there. She could feel his support and appreciated it. He understood what she was fighting for, and that meant so much to her.

Griffen spoke next, backing up what Mia had said. He provided some statistics from the program tests, evidence of the tool's workability. He managed to discuss any lack in the current educational system without maligning efforts that had been made.

He made a case for relieving some of their burden, bringing to attention that Mental Magic was on their side. It was all about educating the youth. He told the group that the purpose was to create confident and involved learners, who grew up to be effective communicators.

Mia perceived a favorable reception from the committee—until James stood up. He looked at Mia with challenge in his eyes. She held her breath, fearing what was next—although certain of what was coming. In a power stance, shoulders back and head high, James studied the group.

His expression when he looked around bordered on pity. He acted as though he was an interested friend, concerned that they'd be misled. Mia marveled at his skill with intimidation. The piercing look at each member made them shrink into their seats.

While he claimed to understand the desire to assist young students, he felt obligated to share the truth. That was odd, coming from a man who could lie without conscience. But only Mia knew that; the parents around the table appeared interested to hear where they'd erred in judgment.

It was a marvel to watch James perform. His skill at manipulation was unrivaled. Mia had experienced it firsthand too many times. The way he garnered trust, how he looked like the epitome of honesty, and the clever way he spoke.

Mia cringed inside. The longer James went on, the more she felt her chances of gaining support slip away. He was good at what he did; she'd give him that. When he was finally finished, Sarah adjourned the meeting, stating that the committee would review all the information then make a recommendation to the board.

Once outside, Mia turned to Ryker, and he put his arm around her. "You were great in there. It's going to be fine...you'll see." She leaned against his strong chest, wishing that James would disappear into a black hole and she wouldn't have to see him anymore.

Griffen and Iris walked out to the parking lot with them. There wasn't much else to say. It was a matter of waiting to see what the advisory committee decided. "We'll see you at the office," Iris said, then left with Griffen.

Mia was about to walk the other way when Ryker stepped in front of her. Looking up, she understood why. James was headed their way. The nerve of that asshole. After undermining her efforts, he thought he could talk to her. She'd give him a piece of her mind, that was for sure.

James came within a foot of her, then smirked. "You won't give up on this delusion that you can help remedial students…will you, Mia?"

The way he said it made her tremble with anger. He spoke to her as if she was a child. While she'd been with him, he'd persisted in making her question her own reality. She'd become anxious, yet he'd put it all on her—until she wondered if she was being too sensitive.

She'd felt like everything she did was wrong, not seeing that he was gradually convincing her of that. It was always her fault when things went wrong, and she'd found herself apologizing. That was before she'd come to her senses and caught on to his tactics.

Mia saw through him; he couldn't do that to her—ever again.

"You heartless bastard," Mia said, stepping closer. "You'd trash a program that could help your own nephew. You'd sacrifice Eddie's future for your own self-centered reasons."

James stiffened. "That boy is not my blood; he can't be. He's my sister's problem. She chose the father, so she has to live with it. It's not my fault he has his father's genes."

James couldn't embrace the idea that he had any faults. He pointed the finger at another, unwilling to see any deficiency on his part. It was remarkable, really. Mia was speechless.

Ryker took Mia's arm. "She has nothing more to say to you. And I suggest you leave her alone, or you'll be dealing with me. Your days of abuse are over." With his arm around Mia, he turned toward the car and walked away, leaving James standing on the asphalt.

"That son of a bitch is on borrowed time," Ryker said. "He'd better back off while he has the opportunity."

*****

For the next few days, it was fairly quiet. Mia wondered if James would finally stop harassing her. She wasn't a woman alone, one he thought he could force into submission. It felt good to have Ryker with her, better than she could have anticipated.

She remembered Ryker putting James in his place. It had been satisfying to watch. But it was too soon for optimism. James might have done too much damage already. It remained to be seen what the advisory board would decide.

If the educational system wouldn't implement her learning tool, Mia could take it to the corporate world. Its use wasn't limited to the young. She planned to expand into other areas once she'd helped students who needed it. It would be valuable in training employees or providing a way to efficiently learn a new technology.

Its uses were only limited by the imagination. Yet Mia couldn't get excited about any of that until she'd achieved what she set out to do. The thought of being blocked from helping children saddened her. She couldn't allow that to happen, and prayed that the parents had seen through James's charade.

It was the end of the week, and Mia sat at her desk, disappointed that she'd had no feedback from the advisory committee yet. It was likely that she'd receive some notice as a courtesy, even though the group's obligation was to the board.

Waiting was difficult, so she tried to immerse herself in work, but with the board's decision hanging in the balance, she found it hard to focus. She welcomed the weekend, hoping that Ryker would be around. She'd like to do something enjoyable, anything to take her mind off worrying about the outcome of the meeting.

Her phone vibrated and she grabbed it, thinking it might be Ryker arranging a time to pick her up. But it was James.

"Unbelievable." Mia shouldn't have answered, but she was furious. "What else could you possibly have to say?"

James chuckled, an irritating sound. "Oh, Mia. Will you never learn? You can't beat me at this game, and you'd be better off cooperating."

"Cooperating?"

"Yes, if you want me to back you up, you'll need to cancel the divorce," James said. "That requires filing a motion to dismiss it. And you only have a couple of weeks left, so all these delays are working against you."

"You've lost your mind."

"No, I don't think so," James said, shifting into a tone of intimidation. "It's in your best interest to come back to me, even though I don't know why I'd even consider taking you back after all you've done."

Mia was too stunned to hang up.

"I'll assist you in running your company, since clearly you're struggling with that," James said. "We can pretend that none of this ever happened. I have a generous spirit, and that's fortunate for you." He paused. "We belong together. No one will love you like I do."

"Fuck off," Mia said, surprising herself.

"Now, now," James said. "I see that you need persuading. I have more photos of you that I am sure your *boyfriend* won't appreciate. I'll expose them publicly, with text messages, emails, private letters…all of it."

Mia floundered to understand. What could he possibly have?

"I'm giving you until Monday to agree to my terms," James said. "Or I'll take what I want my way. And I guarantee that you won't like it."

The call ended, and Mia stared at the phone as if it was a snake. She couldn't think of what to do, how to purge James from her life. If she didn't do it soon, her life would be destroyed. He'd just issued the ultimate threat: do what I say, *or else*. She hadn't forgotten the brutality he'd used before to enforce his wishes. She had no doubt that James intended to take over her company—right after he manipulated himself back into her life.

CHAPTER 10

Ryker sat at his desk, fuming over the ultimatum. Whatever James had planned, he had to be stopped. He assumed he'd get away with bullying, but he'd have to get through Ryker first. The backstabbing way James had of getting what he wanted was infuriating.

If Ryker had his way, he'd beat the crap out of James to teach him a lesson. But that was only wishful thinking. The deadline loomed, making Mia frantic to know what was going to happen. Yet Ryker had other concerns about James.

The asshole was a stalker. The executive protection business was about keeping a client in the public eye safe, which included handling unwanted pursuit behavior. Amanda was an expert in the area, having made it her business to understand such threats.

Ryker headed for her desk to discuss Mia's case. He noticed Jake leaning on Amanda's desk, looking annoyed. Sometimes the two were like siblings, arguing and bickering. "I didn't tell you that," Jake said.

Amanda had her long red hair down, and it waved around her face like a halo of fire. Her blue eyes pierced into Jake. "I don't have time to argue with you. Just let me deal with this and stay out of it." She turned to see Ryker.

"Problem?" Ryker said.

Amanda let out a long breath. "He can be so exasperating. He thinks he knows everything. Can't we put someone else on digital security with me?"

Ryker narrowed his eyes.

"Yes, I know...he's one of the best," Amanda said. "But he's a jackass sometimes."

Ryker sat in the chair beside her desk. He didn't want to get into their differences, figuring they'd work it out. "I want to talk to you about something."

"Mia?"

Ryker had discussed this before. It was why he'd had Amanda take extra steps regarding James. The greater the understanding of his behavior, the better the chance of predicting what he might do, then implementing preventative measures.

"That ex-husband of hers is a piece of work," Amanda said. "He doesn't deal with rejection well. The first line of defense is monitoring Mia's mail, phone calls, emails, gifts, and so on. That way we can pick up any red flags that might be precursors to greater danger."

"I've been watching all of that, culling through all that you send me," Ryker said. "And we tightened protection by keeping an eye on the guy. But his methods are cutthroat. He's making it difficult for me to avoid confrontation."

"As tempting as that might be," Amanda said, "it's better to work toward containment. If you confront James, that could incite more extreme behavior, just what we don't want. He would perceive any confrontation as a challenge and that will piss him off."

"This ultimatum, though," Ryker said. "He will have to realize that Mia isn't going to do what he wants."

"That concerns me," Amanda said. "When violence occurs, it's usually because the pursuer realizes that their fantasy isn't going to happen."

"I intend to stick close to Mia, until we can nail down what that guy is up to." Sooner or later, James would have to come to terms with letting go. Ryker predicted that he'd explode. The only question was: what would he do when that fury boiled up inside?

*****

Over the weekend, Ryker continued Mia's self-defense lessons. He'd tightened security, but that didn't absolve him of training her to defend herself. He showed her more advanced moves and didn't go easy on her.

Mia accused him of being bossy, but he impressed upon her that she must be able to defend against an attacker. Martial arts for sport wasn't the same as learning to evade being a victim, and that included using any means to stop a person intent on harming or killing.

Unpleasant though it may be, such skill was necessary. If Ryker had to bully Mia into competence, then he would. Her life might depend on it.

While Ryker touched, held, and wrestled with Mia, he had to face his feelings for her. He was falling for her yet couldn't let that show. The timing was bad. And personal emotion regarding a client was unacceptable. Whatever his heart urged him to do, Ryker needed to keep things on a professional level.

On Monday, there was no word from James. The hours ticked by, and Ryker kept in touch with Mia. But she'd begun to wonder if the ultimatum had been a bluff. While Ryker waited and watched, he tended to the business of her security.

Caleb and the team were on duty, with orders to report any suspicious activity. Throughout the morning, it was quiet. Mia was at her office, and James was under surveillance. Yet it was impossible to relax about the situation.

While handling Mia's mail, Ryker opened a letter from her bank. It was about her business account. He'd been looking for any communications that could be considered dangerous. But he hadn't been expecting that.

He leapt up from his chair, grabbed his phone, and headed for Mia's office. This couldn't wait.

Mia was in a meeting, and the receptionist asked if it was important enough to interrupt. Ryker told her that it was urgent, then paced the lobby. It wasn't long before Mia emerged with a look of concern. He hated to break the news, but it couldn't be avoided.

"Let's go to my office," Mia said.

Once the door closed, Ryker didn't waste any time. He handed over the letter. Mia read it, and her expression changed. She sank into her chair. "What? Can they do this?"

"Yes, is the short answer," Ryker said. "Your bank has the right to cut you off anytime it wants. The fourteen-day notice is a courtesy. But it makes you wonder why they'd want to lose you as a customer."

"Do you have any idea?" Mia said. "It doesn't give a specific reason." She looked at the letter. "It only says: *if the bank deems you too risky, it can close your account.*"

"It's my understanding that if the bank services a questionable account, they risk getting hit with penalties," Ryker said. "A bank might shut down an account even when a customer isn't doing anything explicitly illegal."

"I'm going to demand to speak with the bank manager," Mia said. "If I don't handle this, my account will be frozen."

Ryker informed Caleb of the issue, and of where he was going. Then he drove Mia to the bank. The manager was busy, so she had to wait. When he was free, she was called into the office. The manager introduced himself and greeted Mia cordially.

"You may call me Leon," he said. "And I must tell you that I regret that the bank is forced to take this action."

Leon played the role of concerned bank manager well. He was respectful and professional, but not helpful.

"This is sudden," Mia said. "May I know the reason for the action?"

"I'm afraid I don't have much information yet," Leon said. "The matter is under investigation. You'll receive more details as they are revealed. But I can tell you that the bank is within their rights to close your account."

After leaving the office, Ryker tried to think of something encouraging to offer. Mia would meet with Griffen and arrange to withdraw the company's funds before the account was frozen.

But that didn't mean another bank would accept her. If one bank had reason for refusal, another might too.

Ryker stepped outside first to make sure it was safe for Mia to exit. Then he walked her back to the car. An unidentified man from the next row made his way over. He didn't look armed or dangerous, but not friendly either.

"Mia Scott?" the man said. When Mia looked up, he handed her a document. "You've been served. This is the summons issued by the court as the first step in a lawsuit." Then he walked away.

Mia looked pale; she leaned against the car and flipped through the pages. "James filed a lawsuit against me. This document tells me when to appear to present my defense, and states that my property can be seized or attached."

Ryker tried to keep his cool, since blowing up wouldn't help. "What's the basis for the lawsuit?"

Mia's shock turned to fury. "James claims that he developed the learning tool, so has distribution rights. That is ludicrous. I'm the one with experience in the tech field. He couldn't write a program if his life depended on it."

"This is just harassment."

"But it could put everything on hold," Mia said. "My company could be hung up in a big mess with the court while this gets resolved." Mia put her hand over her eyes. "Dammit...James wants to steal it all."

Ryker ushered her into the car, not wanting to stick around the parking lot.

"I need a drink," Mia said, which sounded like a good idea.

*****

The downtown bar wasn't far, and it was inside a hotel. Ryker was familiar with the place, so knew it had good security. He took Mia to a table in a corner, where he could watch the activity in the room. Then he flagged a server.

Mia ordered a cocktail, while Ryker stuck to club soda. The lawsuit was a new low for James. His ability to tell lies seemed to have no limit.

Mia was quiet until her drink arrived, then she took a couple of sips before saying anything. "I'll let Griffen know about all of this, and he can set up an appointment with our attorney."

Ryker felt protective. He hated the devious methods that James resorted to.

"I won't go down without a fight," Mia said. "Now it makes sense why the bank doubts my authenticity. It's so unfair."

"James has zero evidence to back up that lawsuit."

"You haven't seen him in a courtroom," Mia said. "I have. And I can tell you that in a legal arena, being in the right isn't enough. James can wreak destruction on my business, and me, before I can get the suit dropped."

"You've been in court before?"

"The divorce," Mia said. "What a nightmare that was."

"He physically abused you; any judge would grant divorce on those grounds."

Mia huffed. "You'd think. Let me enlighten you. I hadn't gone to the authorities and I had no witnesses. When my injuries were severe, I went to the hospital but lied about the cause."

"Why didn't you file any police reports?"

For a moment, Mia didn't answer. She took a gulp of her drink then said, "Many women don't file a report. There's a stigma attached to it. The victim is questioned as though it might be her fault. And there's fear of retribution. An abusive spouse is angered by any report of his actions, so he would go after the woman with more violence than before."

That made Ryker's blood boil. He itched to get his hands on James.

"The judge sided with James," Mia said. "Oh, he granted the divorce. A woman is permitted to leave her husband. But his attitude was that my husband had been treated unfairly."

"That's hard to swallow."

"You were at the meeting the other day," Mia said. "You've seen James in action. Did he look like an abuser to you?"

Ryker just looked at her.

"No, I didn't think so," Mia said. "He is an upstanding citizen, a male who is respected in his profession. A violent man?" She shook her head. "No one believes that of him, not after meeting him."

Mia had another drink, then Ryker took her to dinner. There wasn't much to be done immediately. Her attorney would handle things. But how long would that take, and how much damage would be done before he did?

*****

It seemed that once James attacked, he was relentless. A day went by, and the meeting with the attorney was scheduled. Mia had told Griffen and the team about the new turn of events. They would stick together and get through this. She was assured that she had their support.

The next night, Mia decided to eat dinner at the condo. She didn't feel like going out, needed a break. Ryker was all for that, so broiled steaks. He enjoyed seeing her relax, if only for an evening. After dessert, Mia settled on the sofa to watch a movie.

She checked her messages before deciding what to watch. Ryker's heart skipped a beat when he saw the look on her face. He waited, knowing it couldn't be good.

Mia handed him her phone. He stared at the post about Mia and James, but the words blurred. All he could see was the image. It was a photograph of them together, taken when they'd been a couple.

It was a very sexy picture of Mia engaged in taboo activity with her husband. Ryker couldn't take his eyes off the image. She was naked and in a pose that was beyond risqué.

James was his rival, the crazy man who vied for Mia's attention. And there she was on camera, lusting for her husband and performing an act that didn't bear discussion in mixed company. Ryker felt overwhelmingly possessive.

It was as though Mia was his, and that bond had been violated. It occurred to him that he was jealous. He didn't dare look at Mia, just stared at the post. The caption claimed it was a photo taken from a private album. It had been posted anonymously.

The image was shocking, even to Ryker. In a bedroom, it might not be. But flashed on a screen publicly, it created physical reactions that he couldn't put aside. He didn't understand, didn't know how Mia could have behaved that way with James, the man who had hurt her.

Mia looked up, and her gaze locked with his. Ryker tried to read her emotions but failed. "Is this real? Is this a picture that was taken of *you*...with James? Was it swiped from a personal album?"

Anger flared in Mia's eyes. She leapt up from the sofa and grabbed her phone. "Yeah, I really did that with James...all the time. I liked it. I'm perverted, but you just didn't know that before." Mia raised her hands. "I have to defend myself against you, too? Where does it end?"

"You *were* married to him." Ryker knew the instant he said it that it was like pouring gas on flames.

"Urrrrgh," Mia said, then stamped her feet. "Go ahead, gang up on me. I won't give in, you'll see. I don't care what you believe. Why even ask? You made up your mind the instant you saw that picture." She stormed to her bedroom and slammed the door so hard that the walls shook.

CHAPTER 11

Mia kicked off her shoes, changed into her nightgown, and went to bed. Yet she was too upset to sleep. She fisted her pillow, exasperated. It was impossible to find a comfortable position. She wanted to scream...at *someone*.

She couldn't be more embarrassed by how James had put her on display. If he could think of anything more devastating to do, he surely would. It was more than she should have to endure, and she was at her wits' end.

The burden of it all weighed on her. She'd been pushed to her limits. Now, she was furious with Ryker too. He'd hurt her by not trusting her. But if she had to explain that to him, it defeated the purpose. She'd thought he had faith in her, but she'd been wrong.

The truth hurt, but it was better that she realized it sooner rather than later. That didn't make it any better. Mia had started to believe him. The way he stayed close and seemed to care had made her lower her guard. Yet she should have known better.

Hadn't she had enough experience with men to know that she couldn't depend on them? What did it take for her to not make that mistake again? Had she really been viewing Ryker as a potential boyfriend, a real relationship?

Mia buried her face in her pillow, disappointed in herself. All of this wouldn't hurt so bad if she hadn't deluded herself into thinking that Ryker cared. She was a client, no more than a job to him. She'd best remember that before he broke her heart.

Devastated, Mia stared at the ceiling, trying to figure a way out of the mess. Her life was falling apart, and there didn't seem to be much she could do about it. She hated feeling weak and despised James for putting her in a vulnerable position.

Her injured feelings would heal, but she wasn't sure that she could keep her life glued together. As if things weren't bad enough, she found herself dreaming of Ryker—envisioned being naked in *his* arms.

Reason urged her to block him out, but her body refused to cooperate. Traitor that it was, feelings of desire swamped her, so she hugged a pillow to her chest to quell the sensations. Dammit, why did Ryker have to do that? Couldn't he have trusted her just a little bit more?

*****

At breakfast, Mia maintained the wall of silence.

Wisely, Ryker didn't mention the argument, because if he did, there was no guarantee what her reaction would be. She watched him make waffles and flip the bacon sizzling on the stove.

He had the nerve to be sexy as hell in his jeans and tight shirt. The sleeves clung to his arms, accentuating his biceps. The sight of his wide shoulders and strong back turned her on, and that only made her madder.

It wasn't fair. If Ryker was going to betray her, at least he could be decent enough to be unattractive. Mia looked at her coffee then took a sip. She had to keep her eyes off her *bodyguard*. She couldn't seem to control herself, which was annoying.

It had been a bad idea for Ryker to take the role of close protection and stay at her condo. On the one hand, Mia was safer—but only from external dangers. On a personal level, she was vulnerable as hell. She was being taken advantage of.

With Ryker in the bedroom next to her every night, she couldn't be expected not to feel anything. It irked her. If only she really didn't like him. But he had a charming way about him, and kept his calm, despite her moods.

There was a lot right about Ryker. Too bad he'd messed it up.

Ryker slid the plates onto the table and sat

across from her. He ate his food without comment, then refilled his coffee. If he thought that she was going to apologize, then he was mistaken. He'd let her down and would have to admit it.

Mia finished her waffle, trying to stay tough. It was awkward. Heck, she was eating breakfast with Ryker like he was a roommate—or a lover. For some reason, she felt out of her depth. She'd been angry before, but that hadn't bothered her.

But shutting Ryker out was more difficult than she'd thought.

When the dishes were in the dishwasher, Mia grabbed her purse and waited in the living room for Ryker to drive her to the office. It was going to be a long ride, considering the rift between them. She could take the heat if he could.

Ryker acted as if everything was normal. He wasn't chatty, but he opened the door for her. His professionalism was a stab to the heart. If only he'd been irate; that would show he felt something for her. Mia was down on herself for wanting him to care and struggled to believe that it didn't matter.

At her office, Ryker escorted her inside then stayed as her security. She wished for Caleb but didn't say anything. She'd have to put up with the strained relationship for now. Iris followed her to her desk, and Mia was glad to have someone to talk to.

"You look tired," Iris said. "Didn't you sleep well?"

"You don't know the half of it." Mia told her everything, leaving the worst for last.

"I can't believe Ryker behaved that way," Iris said. "And more shocking is James. That man is a menace."

"It's overwhelming," Mia said. "I have to go in there and tell Griffen this news. It's one thing after the other. Sure, the team has supported me. But how long will that last if this keeps up?"

"It's not your fault. Everyone knows that."

"Do they?" Mia sighed. "I'm not sure anymore. The situation is impossible. Every time I turn around, there's something else. How much can we take…all of us?"

"You're distraught," Iris said. "It will be okay. Griffen is a good manager; he'll share this news in the best light possible. And who knows, the public might side with you, feel your pain…if you know what I mean."

Mia gave her a tiny smile. "Ever the optimist. That's why I love you, Iris."

Iris went with Mia to the manager's office. Griffen listened without reacting, then stated that he'd deal with it. "I'll contact our attorney and schedule a meeting. Meanwhile, he can write a letter to the bank and file a proper response to the lawsuit."

Iris looked at Mia. "See, I told you. Griffen isn't going to abandon ship over the antics of your ex."

"Not a chance," Griffen said. "It isn't the first time that James has tried to back you into a corner. We'll fight him with every resource we have. What we're doing is too important."

Mia felt better after leaving his office. Actions were being taken to calm things down; that was something. She tended to vital tasks, but it wasn't easy to get her mind off the issues she faced. Somehow, she managed to get through the week.

Ryker stuck close, and Mia was civil to him. But the tension between them was palpable.

On Saturday, Ryker told her that he was going to visit his brother—and she was coming with him. "I'm not willing to leave you, and besides, it will be a good change for you. You'll meet his wife and kids, the whole family."

Mia could have argued, but she didn't want to be alone to stew about her problems. Plus, she'd have other people to talk to besides Ryker. It was a warm day, so she dressed in shorts, a cotton top, and sandals. She threw a few things into a straw bag and was ready.

Ryker wore faded jeans and a polo shirt with his jogging shoes. He probably dressed for action, even though it was likely safe with his relatives. Technically, he was on duty, so wouldn't have worn sandals he couldn't run in. Mia was beginning to get to know him.

His brother lived in Chestnut Hill, a neighborhood with family homes. It was a quiet street with many trees and seemed like a good place to raise kids. The brick two-story home had blue shutters at the upstairs windows, and a wide porch with white railings and awnings. It looked like something out of a storybook to Mia, and she imagined the perfect family inside.

Ryker knocked, and when there was no answer, he went in. "We're here!" He turned to Mia. "They're probably on the patio." He led her through the house then out back.

"Hey, man. Glad you could make it."

"This is my brother Ian." Ryker slapped his brother on the back. "And this is his wife Christa."

Mia was greeted with hugs from each. Ian looked like Ryker, except he was shorter and not as muscular. His wife was pretty, with long, dark hair and a friendly smile.

"Sit and relax," Ian said. "What can I get you to drink?"

Ryker asked for a cold beer, and Mia chose white wine, noticing that Christa was drinking some. The backyard was big, with toys strewn about and structures to climb on. Mia sat in one of the patio chairs and sipped her wine.

There were two children in the yard, laughing

and playing. One was a girl about four years old, cute as could be. She wore an outfit made of material that had colorful fish all over it. She screeched with delight as her older brother tackled her and grabbed the ball.

"Those are our kids," Christa said. "Our son is Timmy, and his sister is Chloe. I don't know where they get their energy."

Mia looked at the kids playing outdoors, rolling on the grass, and having fun with the toys. They were fortunate to have the parents they did. Sadness surfaced as Mia thought about her childhood. It had been as different from this as one could imagine.

Ian put his beer on the table, then jogged out to the lawn to wrestle with the kids. "Daddy!" his son said. Then Ian lifted his daughter high in the air until she laughed with delight. The warm scene touched Mia. It was good to see, and she was glad to see children so loved.

Ryker took a swig of beer then went out to join the activities. He tossed a softball to Timmy, staying close to be sure he could catch it. Chloe didn't want to be left out, so she ran up to Ryker and hugged his leg. "Me too. I want to play."

Ryker lifted her in his arms then ruffled her hair. "Oh, you'd beat us all."

He stooped down, placed the ball in her tiny hand, then helped her toss it far enough to get to her brother. The little girl giggled. "Again, Uncle Ryker. Do it again."

The kids played with Ryker, and clearly adored him. Ian came back to the table and sat down. "I'll let them have some time with him. They don't get to see him that often."

Christa talked to Mia, making her feel a part of the family. She shared that Ryker was a year older than Ian, who had chosen a different profession. "He went into medicine and specialized in pediatrics," she said. "He had an issue with his knee from high school sports, so didn't qualify for the military."

While they talked, Ian grilled hamburgers and hot dogs and drank his beer. Ryker seemed to have as much energy as the kids, so kept them entertained. "You have a wonderful family," Mia said. "I'm happy that I got this chance to meet you."

The afternoon proceeded as pleasantly as it started. Christa had made potato salad and brought out dill pickles with other condiments for the meal. Mia helped in the kitchen, really enjoying it. She marveled at how good it felt to be part of a family, even if only for a few hours.

The kids ate hot dogs drowned in ketchup and washed it down with fruit punch. Chloe had tired herself out, so after eating, she curled up on a lounge chair and fell asleep. Timmy grabbed a cookie and ran out to the swing set, ready for more activity.

The boy had dark, wavy hair and big eyes. He reminded Mia of Eddie. He was about the same age and looked much like him. She looked at Ryker's niece and nephew, glad they were happy children. She thought of what would happen if they needed help.

Any child could have a learning disability. Eddie wasn't different from any other boy his age, except he struggled in school. She prayed that she'd succeed in her aim to make life easier for him, and to give him a chance at a future like other children.

After one beer, Ryker switched to iced tea. But there was nothing wrong with his appetite. He ate two burgers with everything on them, then had dessert. He talked with Ian about sports, cars, and other guy things. And he thanked Christa for a great meal.

Mia's attitude had softened. She couldn't help but view Ryker as a father. He was a good uncle, but he could have had a family of his own. The thought of how he'd lost his wife in such a tragic accident pulled at her heartstrings.

Ryker smiled at her, clearly having a good time. "How's your ice cream?"

Mia grinned. "Excellent; I'm going to have seconds."

It was a good day and had been a treat for Mia to meet Ryker's family. She'd bonded with Christa and promised to come back to visit. She meant it, as she'd enjoyed spending time there—more than she would have expected.

Mia had let go of her worries for those few hours. It felt good, and she wasn't anxious to return to the drama of her life. Ryker said his goodbyes, hugging the kids and kissing Christa on the cheek. At the car, he suggested making a day of it.

"I'd like that," Mia said. "I'm not ready to go back."

The Garden District, with its quaint, tree-lined streets, had many pubs, restaurants, and bakeries. It wasn't difficult to find a place to go. Mia suggested the Paris Bistro, a place she'd been to before. She stepped through the glass front door then descended the mosaic tile stairway into the bar.

She was transported to another time and place. The bistro reminded her of Paris in the nineteen thirties, with red leather and velvet upholstery. It had large, ornate mirrors, giving it a warm look. And the décor included beautifully crafted custom metalwork, a tin ceiling, and black-and-white tile floors.

Lunch had been a few hours ago, but Mia wasn't quite ready to eat yet. The bar was a good place to enjoy a glass of chilled Bordeaux blanc with a plate of garlicky escargot. Ryker wasn't too sure about the choice of appetizer but seemed to like it. It took some convincing to get him to try the delicacy.

Conversation between them was still a bit icy, but Mia began to view Ryker differently. She hadn't seen him in a family setting before, and it quite suited him. As much as she tried to fight it, she was drawn to him. It was hard for her to accept that a man might love and admire her.

Mia hadn't experienced authentic love from a man, just the fake kind intended to mislead her. Used to defending herself, it took some adjusting to consider that she might be on safe ground. Ryker's kindness and caring threw her off. She didn't know what to make of it.

"I'm glad you came with me today," Ryker said. "I don't see them often enough. I'll have to correct that. The kids are growing up fast."

"You seem to get along well with your brother."

"In many ways, we're different, but we've always been close," Ryker said.

The server cleared the appetizer plate and brought drink refills. Ryker talked about growing up, scrapes he'd gotten into with Ian, and told stories about the kids. He'd been away when they were born, but he'd made a point to be a part of their life since he'd been home.

When they got hungry, they went to the dining room and had red snapper with fava beans. It didn't seem to matter that Mia was still in shorts and sandals. The atmosphere was elegant but not stuffy. She enjoyed Ryker's company and was pleased to spend the day with him.

After the meal, Ryker took her down one flight of stairs to the stylish jazz café. Musicians played selections from the Jazz Age. It had started out as a day away, time with the family—but it had turned into a date. And it was very romantic.

On the way home, Mia shared more than she'd intended to. She talked about Ryker's family and how she'd lacked any male role model while growing up. "I think having a father to look up to is important."

"I couldn't agree more," Ryker said. "Those kids are lucky to have such a great dad. Ian dotes on them, and Christa, too."

Mia wondered if she'd misread Ryker the night before. She was touched by his sentiment and was drawn to him. He was a good man. Yet she resisted letting him into her heart. There was still the matter of him believing the worst about her.

At her condo, Ryker locked the door behind them and shut the drapes. "No need to have anyone spying on us." He smiled. "It's been known to happen. Don't you watch spy movies?"

"You mean the guy in the building across the

way with a telescope?" Mia said with a laugh. "Sure, who hasn't seen that in a film?"

Ryker stood by the window looking at her. The soft light in the room made him look impossibly desirable.

"About last night..." Mia said.

Ryker came closer. "Yes, was there something you'd like to say?"

"I can't believe you had so little faith in me."

"The ropes...the chains?" Ryker's eyes sparkled. "You have to admit, it was a bit incriminating."

Standing so close, Mia's body warmed and her skin tingled. "It was fake," she whispered in a deep, sensual voice. "It was my face but some other woman's body."

Ryker looked into her eyes, and she melted. "In my defense, I haven't seen you naked. It was an honest mistake."

Mia was swept up in the emotion. Her attraction to Ryker was strong, rapidly becoming too powerful to ignore. His kindness had pierced her defensive shield. He was a fierce warrior with a kind heart, a deadly combo if there ever was one. When he stroked his fingertips along her jaw, she felt her resistance crumbling.

CHAPTER 12

Ryker ran his fingertips along Mia's jaw and sensed the last of her anger melt away. The challenge in her eyes was replaced by desire, and her emotion ignited his passion. He placed his palm on Mia's cheek, feeling the softness of her skin.

Mia had been by his side all day, shared family closeness, and it had felt so right. Ryker was seeing things clearly for the first time. She belonged with him, and he wanted her by his side for more than just an afternoon.

"I trust you," Ryker whispered. "You were married. I can't fault you for the past."

Mia didn't defend herself, as if finally realizing that she didn't need to.

Ryker dragged his thumb over her lips. "But...I can get jealous."

Mia's eyes widened. "Were you...*jealous*?"

"It killed me to see you with another man." Ryker was desperate for her touch, so he reached to pull her close—yet Mia flinched.

Remembering that she'd been abused was a knife to Ryker's heart. There was no telling what she'd suffered at the hands of the man she'd been married to. "I wouldn't hurt you," he said, looking deep into her lovely brown eyes.

Mia gazed at him, then tears welled in her eyes. "Promise?"

"I promise." Ryker would give his life before hurting her or permitting any harm to come to her.

Mia was so beautiful, a loveliness that flowed from the inside out. He drank in the sight of her. Her hair was messy from the day's activities, and she was in shorts with a light top. She looked so touchable, so irresistible. Ryker imagined pulling down her shorts, craved seeing her naked, and having her in his arms.

Deep emotion welled up inside, leaving Ryker weak with desire. He wanted Mia, could hardly endure another moment without her. All he wanted to do was love her, to show her how much he cared—to share intimate moments with her. He wanted to strip her naked and ravage her with abandon.

With his arms around Mia's waist, Ryker pulled her against his chest, relieved that she didn't resist. He was so close that he could feel her breath on his skin, breathe in her sweet perfume. He leaned down then touched his lips to hers.

It was their first kiss, sweet yet electric. Mia

pressed closer, so Ryker kissed her again. The fervor of the encounter sent heat radiating through his body. He dug his hand in her hair, holding her to kiss her more. The tentative kiss sparked passion.

Ryker licked over the seam of her lips, then dipped his tongue inside. Mia accepted his advance and responded in kind. Any reserve quickly dissolved, and the kiss was deep, filled with longing. The feel of her lips, the taste of her mouth, the excitement of holding her in his arms sent a thrill straight to his loins.

He wanted only to please her, to take her away to a secret place that only they could share. He kissed her again, longer this time, without wanting to release her. Mia raked her fingers through his hair then wrapped her hands behind his neck to pull him closer.

Ryker couldn't get close enough; he couldn't kiss her long enough or deep enough. The strength of the attraction bonded them, in a way he had no control over. The kisses were hot, and her body against his even hotter.

When Ryker slid his hands over her curves, Mia made a sexy sound in her throat, driving him crazy. He nibbled her earlobe, then raked his tongue along the side of her neck. He kissed her cheek, her eyelids, then under her jaw. It was impossible to gain satisfaction, because the more he kissed her, the more he wanted.

*****

Mia closed her eyes, just feeling, only desiring. The sensations Ryker created with his hot kisses made her weak in the knees. She kissed back, touching his hard body, inhaling his male scent. There was no holding back; she didn't want to.

With Ryker's hands on her, his lips burning against her sensitive skin, Mia wanted only to have him in every way possible. She reached behind and dragged her palms down his back, then cupped his firm ass. Her blood boiled with desire, and a spike of need pierced deep to her core.

"Please...please." Mia gasped, unsure what she was pleading for. But she hoped that Ryker would know, that he would sweep her into the ecstasy that threatened to overtake her.

Ryker lifted Mia into his arms then carried her to his bedroom. Invading his privacy felt so decadent, yet so good. This was the room where he slept, where he had been so close every night. But now she was with him, in his embrace.

When Ryker lowered her feet to the floor, Mia didn't move away. She put her arms around his neck, anxious for more kissing, fearing he would disappear, and she'd wake up from this wonderful dream. She tipped her head up, and Ryker kissed her with a depth of passion that conveyed his need for her.

Impatiently, Ryker undressed her. He yanked down her shorts and underwear, then she stepped out of them. He pulled off her top, taking a moment to gaze at her breasts. Her nipples were so stiff they ached. Thankfully, he undid her bra and took one nipple into his mouth.

"So beautiful," Ryker whispered, then sucked on her other nipple, leaving the first one abandoned—but not for long. He rolled one nipple between his thumb and finger, while sucking and licking the other.

Wetness seeped between Mia's legs, and she trembled with need. Ryker's mouth spiraled her arousal, tempting her to give in to a climax. Then he stopped, pressing his mouth to her collarbone, her neck, her cheek. He was still clothed, yet she was so naked.

Ryker drew back the covers then lifted Mia to the bed. He shoved his jeans down, then kicked off his shoes and stepped free. She gazed at his lean thighs, drooling to feel them against her. She stared as Ryker pulled his shirt off, then removed his briefs, releasing his erection.

Heat consumed Mia as she looked at his naked form. Ryker was a stud in clothes, but even more without them. She ogled at his broad shoulders, muscled arms, narrow waist. Then she lingered, staring at his hard cock. She tried to breathe but found it impossible.

A thin line of hair went down his flat belly, and a thatch of dark hair was at the base, drawing her attention to his heavy balls. "Ryker..."

When he stepped close, Mia fisted his cock, relishing the heat and hardness. Ryker moaned and pushed his hips forward. Then he got on the bed to straddle her, but he didn't satisfy her greatest need yet. Instead, he lowered his head and kissed her most sensitive area.

With deftness and expertise, Ryker tended to her, licking and sucking just right. "You taste like honey." Mia didn't answer; she couldn't talk. Her body tingled with pleasure, and when Ryker spiraled his tongue around her tight clit, she came unglued.

A delicious orgasm washed through Mia, propelling her into a cloud of pleasure then causing her to fall limp in the aftermath. But instead of sating her, the intense moment only made her want more. She reached for Ryker, and he crawled up to her for a kiss.

Mia could taste her juices on his tongue and smell his desire. She raked her fingernails down his back then reached around to cup his balls, rolling them in her hands. "I want to taste you too."

Ryker moved up, so she could reach. With her eyes half closed, Mia licked up and down his erection, craving his heat. She wanted more, as the sensual treat only served to stir her desire. She put the tip of his cock in her mouth, moaning with pleasure, then rolling her tongue over his sensitive spot under the rim.

Mia moved over him and sucked, as Ryker cupped her breasts then fingered her nipples. It was all too much, making her unravel and take him deeper into her mouth.

Ryker growled from deep in his throat. He reached to the side table and retrieved a condom from the drawer. He rolled it on then looked into her eyes.

"I want you...so much," Ryker said, then kissed her lips. With his knee, he pushed her thighs wider. Then he eased into her.

His thick cock stretched her as he pushed inside, and the sensation was heavenly. Mia panted and arched her back to take him deeper. Ryker stroked, escalating her pleasure. As he went deep, Ryker moaned, then he pulled back. He nearly pulled out of Mia, but not quite, making her whimper.

Ryker moved in a rhythm, pushing her closer to the precipice. He kissed the mounds of her breasts and his mouth grazed her jaw. He was gentle yet so strong and powerful. The world fell away, and only Ryker existed, just his touch and the feel of him inside her.

Mia opened to him, taking all that he would give. She trusted him, so let go of any reserve. He had her body and her heart. There was no going back. Ryker was hot, fierce—and he was *hers*. In that special moment, Mia transcended space and time.

She was closer to Ryker than she'd been with anyone. It was as though she was one with him; there was no separation. She felt his need, sensed his desire, and wanted to give him satisfaction. Her body was warm, her lower belly tight in anticipation of climax.

Yet it didn't end. Ryker's lust seemed to have no limits. He devoured her with his kisses and touches, while he stroked without end. Sex was long and slow, delicious and nearly unendurable. Then the pace shifted to fast and hard. Mia met him thrust for thrust.

Sweating and panting, Mia's sensations crested. With a deep thrust, Ryker stilled against her, his face nuzzled in her hair. Losing all control, Mia shattered in his arms, crying out his name as the waves of a powerful orgasm exploded within her.

Ryker moaned loudly, then released into her, in the grip of his own climax. He came long and hard, finally collapsing against her. When he rolled to the side, he cradled Mia in his arms. She felt so protected, so adored.

She draped her leg over Ryker's thighs and rested her head against his shoulder. She put her arm around his waist, holding him close as he stroked her hair. She closed her eyes, soaking in the intimacy, the boundless pleasure—and she didn't want to let him go.

CHAPTER 13

Mia was an amazing woman. She was so sexy that once was not enough. Ryker had made love with her several times throughout the night. Yet he wanted more, because those intimate moments had made it clear what she meant to him.

Ryker hadn't slept much. He still woke up early Sunday morning with Mia's back pressed against his chest. The spoon position was tender, and she was so warm, so soft. He envisioned what it would be like to have Mia next to him for the rest of his life.

That Ryker had another chance at love seemed too good to be true. He'd been heartbroken over the loss of his wife. He'd immersed himself in work, but there had been no way to heal emotionally. He was devoted to his career, so hadn't been looking for a relationship.

Mia was special. After holding her in his arms and sharing such closeness, Ryker was lost to her allure. He hadn't conceived meeting a woman he wanted to share his life with. He hadn't thought that was possible. Loving again was a gift, and he cherished Mia.

Ryker had wondered if he could ever move on, if he could open his heart to another love or find a woman who could understand. He would miss Amy, but it didn't have to be in a debilitating way. She'd had a kind heart and would have wished a love-filled life for him.

Amy and his marriage to her had partially molded Ryker into the man he was. It was a part of his life that he wouldn't forget. Yet his heart told him that Amy wouldn't want him to be alone or spend the rest of his days heartbroken.

Because of Mia, it was possible to heal, and the journey through life with her was one he longed for. Ryker would always love Amy, but the heart seemed to have an infinite capacity. He found that caring for Mia brought joy to his life, without taking anything away from his first love.

Ryker was sure of two things. He loved Mia deeply, and he was one lucky guy for having found love twice in his life. He closed his eyes and pulled Mia closer, breathing in her scent. He was content to be with her, to listen to her steady breathing, and know that she was safe in his arms.

It was a while before Mia stirred, as it had been a long night. She stretched, then nestled against Ryker, stirring his arousal. "How long have I slept?" She yawned and turned in his arms.

"Not long enough," Ryker said. "I didn't give you much quiet time last night."

Mia gave him a sensual smile. "If I want quiet time, I can sleep alone in my bed." She touched Ryker's cheek. "I don't care if I ever sleep again, as long as it means I can be with you."

"You know how to flatter a guy."

"Flattery is something you don't need," Mia said. "You were fantastic last night. I'll be dreaming about you from now on."

Ryker brushed a strand of hair away from her face. "You won't have to be dreaming about me. I'll be right by your side."

Mia's eyes glistened. "Do you mean that?"

"I mean every word," Ryker said. "In case you thought I only said it last night in the heat of passion, I'll say it again." He tipped her chin up and kissed her lips. "I love you."

"That's a good thing, because if I loved you any more, my heart would burst."

Ryker grinned. "Do you always argue and bicker with a man you love?"

"You can't resist teasing, can you?" Mia said. "I wouldn't know. I haven't been in love before."

Ryker looked into her lovely brown eyes, waiting for her to explain.

"Oh, I've been seduced, charmed...even married," Mia said. "But I haven't felt what I feel for you for any other man."

"Now you're trying to boost my ego."

"It needs boosting?" Mia slid her hand down his arm and along his thigh. Then she reached between them to fist his erection.

Ryker wanted her more than he had before, wondering if he'd want her more by the day and if there was any limit. If there was, he didn't think he'd reach it anytime soon.

Mia pushed him onto his back and climbed on top. She gave him a passionate kiss, then licked down his chest. Ryker moaned from the sensations, and realized the feeling was more than physical—his heart was involved.

"I love you," Ryker said from deep in his throat, unable to tell her often enough.

"I'll show you how I feel about you," Mia said, then lowered over his hard cock. Ecstasy swamped him, and Ryker embraced the woman he adored. The way she opened her heart, gave of herself, left no doubt about how she felt.

Mia reached her climax at the same time he did and, with a sweet groan, collapsed on top of him. Draped over his body, she said, "I never knew it could be like that."

Ryker rubbed her back. "I'll have to let you be on top more often."

Mia looked into his eyes. "No, I don't mean that. I was talking about all night...everything. The way you made love to me, the caring, the closeness..."

"The love?"

"Yes, the love," Mia said. "I just...didn't know what I was missing."

Mia's bathroom tub was a Jacuzzi, so she suggested taking a warm bath. It would ease her delicious aches. Ryker figured that she had to be sore after what he'd put her through. He filled the tub and got in after her.

The hot water and pulse of the jets felt good. That was something Ryker could get used to, along with other things. He planned to spoil Mia. If she thought that last night had been unique, she'd soon realize how much love he had to share with her.

Mia sank down in the water and sighed, but she didn't stay down long. Under the water, she tickled Ryker with her toes, so he grabbed her foot. Soon they were splashing water and making a mess. Reaching across, Ryker pulled her to him for a kiss, then he tickled her.

Mia giggled. "That's not fair. You tricked me." Under the water, she reached for him, distracting him from any more tickling.

"That feels too good," Ryker said. "If you keep that up, you'll be in trouble."

"You must know by now that I can handle any trouble you dish out."

Ryker pulled her up to position her over his

hips. Then he fingered her until she panted softly in his arms, before giving in to a sweet orgasm. He loved watching her face during her climax. Her pleasure was beautiful, and he was honored to be the one responsible for it.

Mia wrapped her arms around his neck and leaned her head on his chest. "I better get out while I have any strength left."

While watching Mia dry off then put on a robe, Ryker grabbed a towel to wrap it around his waist. "I'll meet you in the kitchen for coffee," he said.

After drying, Ryker pulled on jeans and a shirt, then went to make the coffee. God knew he could use some. Mia took longer to get ready, so by the time she appeared, he was on his second cup. She wore pink jeans and a cream-colored blouse that he had the urge to take off.

Mia accepted a cup of coffee, then sat across from him. "If we plan to stay out of bed, we should probably go somewhere."

"I could use some food. How about breakfast?"

"I'm famished," Mia said. "I'm not picky about where we go, as long as there's hot food and lots of it."

Ryker had a place in mind that wasn't far. His stomach growled as a reminder of how long it had been since dinner.

Mia looked out the window. "It's such a

beautiful day. I want to go out and enjoy it."

Ryker was glad it was Sunday, so he didn't have to be anywhere. He could spend the day with Mia. It was a new day and a new start. He had contemplated spending a lot of time with Mia; creating a life with her seemed possible.

Yet there were hurdles to get over. It wouldn't be easy. Ryker wondered if things could really work between them. But he remained convinced that the relationship would endure, that Mia was meant to be in his life. And he'd do all he could to make her happy.

*****

The restaurant had lunch fare as well as breakfast. Since Mia had slept late and they'd had a leisurely start to the day, it was convenient that the place offered brunch. Ryker got a table by the window, which was good for people-watching, then grabbed menus.

It didn't take long for Ryker to decide. He chose a waffle topped with huevos rancheros. He figured that would fill the hole in his stomach. Mia was more reasonable and ordered French toast with strawberries. The food arrived promptly, and the instant the plates were put on the table, they dug into the food.

When Ryker came up for air, he noticed Mia watching him. "What...you haven't seen a man eat before?"

Mia smiled. "Uh, not like that. You inhaled."

"And it's your fault."

"Guilty as charged," Mia said, then took a sip of juice. "Can I ask you something?"

"Sure."

"Last night was…unforgettable," Mia said. "But I can't help wondering where we go from here."

"Wherever it is," Ryker said, "I'd like it to be together."

"I want that too." Mia looked into his eyes. "Yet…are you ready to face the future with me. I mean, can you move forward?"

"If you are talking about losing my wife…then, yes, I can," Ryker said. "I've thought about it, a lot. And I want what we have. You're precious to me."

Mia's eyes were moist, and she dabbed at them with a napkin.

"I lost my wife and it nearly destroyed me," Ryker said. "The future we'd hoped to share was gone…in the blink of an eye." He reached for her hand. "But you give me hope that love can be a part of my life again."

There wasn't any more Ryker could say. He'd opened his heart, something he hadn't thought he could do again. Mia's love meant everything. He'd lost one love and didn't intend to lose another. Whatever came next, he was determined to protect her from danger—and to face the future with her by his side.

When breakfast was over, Mia suggested spending the day together. It was the weekend, so any pressing issues would have to wait. Ryker wasn't big on museums, so was glad to hear that she preferred to spend time outdoors.

Philly had no lack of things to do, but Mia enjoyed walking the streets of Center City. It was her hometown, just like it was Ryker's, so she knew her way around. After strolling and chatting for hours, they stopped for a snack. After continuing on their way, they stopped at a couple of pubs to sample local brews.

Ryker hadn't had so much enjoyment from doing a lot of nothing before. His life had been filled with activity since he'd been home and had been centered around battle when he'd been away. Relaxing for a day hadn't been on the agenda, yet it was pleasant to do with Mia.

In the late afternoon, they ended up at Fairmount Park for a walk under the park's canopy of trees. Ryker held Mia's hand as they made their way along the Schuylkill River trail. Then they sat for a while on an available bench.

Mia looked serious. "It's been a wonderful day, but it hasn't made my problems go away. You've heard that life is messy. Well, whoever said that must have meant mine."

"But doesn't it matter who is by your side?"

"You *are* a romantic," Mia said. "That's a part of you that I like. Still, my company is on the verge of going under. My ex is crazed and won't be satisfied with anything less than my physical and emotional devastation."

"That is bad."

"And…I still don't have a car," Mia said, with a twinkle in her eye. "That's the worst. I lost my Audi."

"You haven't lost your sense of humor."

"Not yet," Mia said, "but it's not over. "When I grew up in foster care, I looked forward to the day that I could be on my own. Yet in my adult life…I've made some bad choices."

Ryker pulled her into his arms to kiss her, and the touch of her lips warmed his heart. "I think that has changed. I'm going to be the best choice you've made…I promise."

CHAPTER 14

The next morning, Mia sat at her desk thinking about Ryker. The weekend had been more wonderful than she could have imagined. Yet she resisted the love that was at her doorstep. The sensual interludes had allowed her to see into Ryker's heart.

But that didn't wipe away old fears. If Mia followed her heart then her defenses would be gone. She'd worked so hard for her independence, and was tired of being pushed around. Marrying an abuser had been scary.

James had been so nice at first. But he had an enormous ego and expected everything to go his way. If it didn't, then he would make it so. A dozen red roses or a night on the town had been tools to control her.

Yet James would resort to any method to maintain his position of power and dominance. That included demeaning Mia in an effort to gain the upper hand, and physical abuse if that didn't get the result. He'd stopped short of threatening her with a weapon, though he might be compelled to go to that length.

Mia shuddered, as she recalled her fear of how far James would go. He could be so charming yet turn into an ugly man, and a threat to her safety. Growing up, she'd fought too hard for survival to allow the pattern to continue.

It made her sick to think of being married to James. Yet she considered that she was one of the lucky ones. She'd had the resources to leave him, and she had. The hard part had been forgiving herself. For a long while, she couldn't understand how she'd ended up with a violent man.

Going forward, the worst part was being able to trust herself and her choices. But she'd learned about the type of personality that she'd been dealing with. The actions James took, his behavior and motives, had become clear.

It was horrifying, but that knowledge had prevented Mia from going back, enabled her to turn a deaf ear to his pleas and to ignore his tactics. Since filing for divorce, James had poured on the charm. It seemed that he assumed a promise of romance and love might do the trick, if he was patient.

Only that hadn't worked. Recently, James had exhibited signs of desperation, and his actions had been more brutal. When Mia thought about James, anxiety riddled her belly. He could have harmed her more severely than he had. Recently, he could have caused physical injury by bombing her car, making her wonder if he would feel any remorse for such an act.

Mia had a right to be cautious, and a reason to be afraid. But Ryker was so different from her ex, and unlike any man she'd known. He was kind and caring, even gentle, yet had a warrior's heart. She was certain that he would protect her if it was within his power.

With James, there had been warning signs that Mia had failed to heed. She wasn't so naïve anymore. But there were no indications that Ryker was anything like James. He couldn't be—because Mia loved him. If he let her down after she'd placed her faith in him, she couldn't imagine recovering.

Mia recalled the special moments with Ryker, cherishing the feeling of love and intimacy. She believed that he loved her. While her mind nagged at her to be careful, her heart guided her closer. He'd promised that he would be the best choice she'd made. Could Mia trust that vow was the truth?

*****

One day, Mia went shopping with Iris. The tech event coming up was a big deal, so required a new outfit. "I have to look sharp," Mia said. "The cameras will be on me."

"You can be sure that will be the case," Iris said. "You are not only a business role model, you've become a fashion icon, too."

"I think you're exaggerating."

"Only a little," Iris said. "We have to shop anyway, because I need something to wear. My closet isn't nearly as stuffed as yours."

"Let's go to Liberty Place," Mia said. "We can start at Bloomingdale's then work our way through."

In the lobby, Caleb escorted them to the car. He and his team had the shift while Ryker was at headquarters. He'd had to devote a couple of days to setting up security for the upcoming event.

Finding the right outfit was no simple task. But after trying on endless possibilities in various stores, Mia selected tasteful business attire. She chose a pencil skirt in soft material with a black and white pattern, then paired it with a silky ivory blouse. A short, tailored black jacket with piping around the edges completed the look.

Iris wouldn't be a speaker at the event, so could be more flexible in how she dressed. Suits and jackets tended to overwhelm her petite frame. After looking through the racks, she found a peach-colored dress that fit just right. It had a narrow belt and the hem fell below the knee.

"Before we look for shoes," Mia said, "I need a break." A coffee shop in the mall offered drinks and pastries, so they stopped there.

While sipping her latte, Iris chatted about what

had been happening in her life. "I'm very involved in the company, since we are at a crucial point. But I have been on a date recently."

"Really? Is he anyone I know?"

"No, he's a guy in my building," Iris said. "I met him in the lobby. I kept running into him, and we'd talk a bit. We went out last week, just to dinner."

"And...is he worth a second date?"

"We'll see," Iris said. "I'll take it slow. How about you? After the weekend, you came in all starry-eyed. We haven't had a chance to catch up. What's happening with Ryker?"

Mia couldn't hide being in love. "We've been intimate."

Iris smiled. "No more separate bedrooms?"

"He's won my heart," Mia said, then frowned. "Do you think I'm making a mistake? I mean, I'm still fending off the last man I hooked up with."

Iris waved her hand. "That is completely different. Ryker is...well, he's not James."

"I know that, but I still worry."

"You need to stop that," Iris said. "I've been around Ryker enough to tell that he's good for you. And he is gorgeous."

Mia laughed. "You would point that out. He's completely irresistible. And he's a good man. I didn't think that was possible to find."

"You really are a cynic," Iris said. "Get over it.

James was a mistake, but it doesn't have to ruin your life."

"You make it sound so easy," Mia said. "And James is still trying to ruin my life. It makes it difficult to move on."

Iris shook her head. "The guy is a lunatic. I can't believe the stunts he's pulled."

"You're worried too, aren't you?"

"I'm just glad you have protection," Iris said. "Your ex is too unpredictable for my taste. And he's out of line with those fake photos."

"I only hope that's the end of it." Mia doubted that it would be, though.

"James doesn't like losing control," Iris said. "And your divorce will be final soon, which has to be driving him mad. I'd keep your eye on him if I were you."

*****

Mia was in the hotseat. The tech event was rapidly approaching, and she hoped to calm investors with her presentation at the podium. Most of her company's investors had stayed with her, but it was uncertain if that could continue.

Griffen was managing Mental Magic's affairs. He'd met with their attorney then informed the team that actions were being taken. The attorney had responded to the lawsuit, which bought some time. And he'd dealt with the bank but was only granted a short extension. That week, he was attempting to secure better banking options for the company.

Midweek, Ryker picked Mia up after work, but had to drop by headquarters on the way to dinner. Black Swan occupied a long warehouse with an office complex at one end. On various occasions, Mia had been on the premises, but only in the gym facilities for self-defense lessons.

She hadn't toured the inside, although it appeared to be an average business office—even if those who worked there were anything but average. The lobby had a few chairs and a table with magazines. An attractive woman in her thirties typed on a keyboard at reception.

Ryker motioned toward the woman as he walked by. "This is Maddie." Then he nodded. "This is our client Mia Scott."

Maddie had long brown hair that was tied back and wire-rimmed glasses. She was pretty, but all business. "It's nice to meet you. I hope we're doing a good job for you."

"So far," Mia said, then followed Ryker down the hallway. "She seems like a nice person."

"Smart and efficient," Ryker said. "That's why we hired her. She takes care of intake forms and some of the client issues...takes some of the workload off the rest of us."

Inside a large space were several desks, and there were stacks of paper and folders strewn around. It was late, and it appeared that some people had already left for the day. Or they were working in the field. From what Mia understood, a large part of protection was active and not desk work.

When Ryker got to his desk, he looked across the room. "Hawke...what are you still doing here?"

Mia turned to see a tall, muscular guy in jeans and a t-shirt. He was clearly SEAL material. He had the look of confidence, and his physical fitness wasn't open to question. When he looked at her, Mia noticed how blue his eyes were.

Hawke strolled over, holding hands with a woman much shorter than he. She had dark blond hair and big brown eyes. Although she was pretty, she struck Mia as a studious type.

"I haven't had the pleasure of meeting you," Hawke said. "I run this operation with Ryker. You can call me Hawke." He turned to look at the woman he was with. "And this is Emilia."

It was obvious to Mia that the two were in love. The look that passed between them couldn't be mistaken for anything else. She shook hands with each. "I'm Mia Scott, founder of Mental Magic," she said for Emilia's benefit.

"Hawke doesn't talk much about clients," Emilia said, "with confidentiality and all. But I would have recognized you anyway. I've seen your picture a lot lately."

"That's unfortunately true," Mia said. "And the news hasn't been favorable much of the time." While Hawke and Ryker discussed business, Mia got to know Emilia. She learned that she was a scientist who developed medicines to cure rare diseases. From the start, she liked her and hoped that she'd be able to get to know her better.

Hawke took Emilia's hand, his possessive side showing. "I'm off to socialize. Emilia and I are meeting her friend Tia and a guy she's dating. But I'm glad to meet you."

"I've heard so much about the team," Mia said. "It's good to put a face with a name."

"You would have soon, anyway," Hawke said. "The team will be covering your tech event. We won't be obvious about it, but I'm sure we would have met then."

Listening to Hawke gave Mia confidence. The way he spoke and his attitude made her feel like part of the team and gave her every reason to rely on their protection.

"We'll do whatever it takes to make sure you're safe," Hawke said. "Events bring unique challenges, but we're up to the task." As further reassurance, he told a story about protection. It seemed that another client was a celebrity.

At a performance, an avid fan who had been stalking the performer leapt onto the stage. The security guard in charge of close protection intercepted, sweeping the performer over his shoulder and carrying her offstage, while fans raged and threw items. "But the client was ushered to safety before any harm came to her," Hawke said.

"I'm impressed," Mia said.

"The point was to assure you that we have many alternatives and ways to protect you," Hawke said. "We start with the most direct and the least likely to bring harm to anyone. But we'll escalate the defense as required; you can be assured of that."

Emilia leaned her head against Hawke's arm. "Okay, *hero*...I'm sure Mia doesn't doubt the team. But I'm starving, so..."

Hawke held up his hand. "I'll see you again. Take care of her, Ryker." Then he left with his sweetheart.

"That was quite a story," Mia said.

Ryker laughed. "Yeah, Hawke likes to tell that one. I was the close protection agent who carted the client to safety. But he didn't mention my name...wouldn't want me to get a big head or anything."

Mia laughed too. "It's not funny, but I can't help envisioning you throwing a client over your shoulder like a sack of potatoes."

Ryker picked up the stuff he'd stopped by to

get, then checked the computer. "We can go. Are you hungry?"

"Of course," Mia said, "and I know you are."

"I'm always hungry."

Ryker's statement made Mia think of more than food. Since the weekend, he had slept next to her—if what they did could be described as sleep. He stirred emotions within her that she hadn't known were possible, and she couldn't seem to get enough of him.

Ryker took her to an Italian place with white tablecloths, quaint wooden chairs, and fresco paintings on the plaster walls. It was a cozy setting and sparked romance. But then, any place Ryker took her would seem romantic.

Over garlic bread and lasagna, Mia talked about her situation. The tech event approached, yet there had been no communication from Sarah at the advisory council. That meant the Board of Education hadn't made any decision.

"Something needs to happen," Mia said. "The summer is important. It's the time for remedial students to catch up, before the exams in the fall."

Ryker seemed to understand. "I hope you get word soon. As far as the event goes, I can assure you of good security. I already have the team scoping out the building in advance, for planning purposes."

"I feel better having your protection," Mia said.

"I should breathe a sigh of relief that James has quieted down. Those scandalous pictures were the last I've heard from him. Yet I'm afraid to hope, to allow myself to think that he will leave me alone."

Ryker didn't comment, as he was clearly too wise to assume danger had passed. Mia changed the subject, since there wasn't anything she could do about her problems right then. She was with Ryker and wished to treasure the evening with him. And whatever she faced…at least she wouldn't be alone.

CHAPTER 15

Mia ate and chatted, not overly focused on the tight spot she was in. But Ryker's gut told him that James wasn't about to go away quietly. That type had to have the last word. It wasn't over yet, but he didn't have the heart to tell Mia. She'd had a welcome break from the onslaught of harassment.

If only Ryker could put an end to the threats and torment, but he hadn't been able to get his hands on James yet. He had a feeling that day would come, because James was pushing his luck. And it wasn't the creep's style to back off.

It was infuriating that Ryker couldn't be with Mia. There was too much standing in the way, and his main rival was her crazy ex. He hadn't vied for a woman before, but if he had, this isn't the way he'd have imagined it.

Battling with some insane dude who didn't have the guts to face him was unacceptable. James would make a mistake, and Ryker would be there to take him apart. Meanwhile, he had Jake and Amanda digging for more information.

There had to be something that Ryker had

missed. James was too respectable and charming on the surface. Knowing about James's abusive nature, and hearing sickening details from Mia, was like a neon sign.

A guy who was capable of such atrocities didn't start yesterday. So that meant James had things in his past that he didn't want known. Ryker would bet on it. He just had to discover what it was, and he needed to find out *soon*.

Ryker had stopped eating, so Mia looked at him. "Did I ruin your appetite?"

"I don't know if that's possible," Ryker said. "I was just thinking…I have the social platforms, plus your email being monitored. There hasn't been a report of anything new. Have you seen anything suspicious?"

"I stopped looking," Mia said. "It was too upsetting. I asked Iris to tell me if there is anything I should know. Until after the event, I need to keep away from the noise. It really gets to be too much…James *and* everything else."

"That's smart." Ryker liked any idea that kept her away from trouble. "You have others looking out for you, so you're able to focus on more important things."

He looked into Mia's huge, dark eyes. She meant so much to him. Although he hadn't asked for a commitment, Mia was his woman. A sense of possessiveness filled him. When the timing was better, he'd ask the right questions.

For now, Mia had enough on her mind, and it was Ryker's business to keep her safe. Yet looking at her, drinking in her beauty like water in a desert, Ryker thought of other things besides danger. He stared at her perfect lips as she slipped a bite into her mouth.

Mia noticed and looked back. Desire flared in her eyes, and she reached under the table to rub his knee. Her gentle touch made him remember holding her naked, as he'd done many times in recent days. He couldn't get enough, and she seemed just as willing.

Ryker put his arm around her then kissed her lips. "Enjoying yourself?"

"Mmm, yes I am," Mia said. "The food here is really good."

"Should I order dessert?" Ryker rubbed his fingertips over her arm and thrilled at the lust he saw in her expression.

"Dessert sounds good," Mia said. "But I'm kind of full right now. Maybe by the time we get home, I'll be ready."

Ryker's blood heated and his pants tightened. "I'm looking forward to that." He couldn't look to the future, because that was uncertain. But he had another precious night with her, and he certainly wasn't going to waste it.

On the way home, Mia kept her hand on his

thigh, spiking Ryker's arousal higher. He kept his eyes on the road but was glad he didn't have far to go. Sex in the car was tempting, but unwise. As exciting as that might be, it wasn't safe.

As long as danger lurked, Ryker had to keep his wits about him. He wouldn't be able to relax and focus until he had Mia securely inside her condo. He wouldn't take a chance with her safety for the sake of momentary pleasure. Some other day, there would be an opportunity for that.

In protection mode, Ryker followed procedure to ensure that it was safe outside. Then he escorted Mia through the parking lot, keeping his eyes and ears open. Things were quiet, so he guided her inside her condo then locked the door.

With the deadbolt securely in place, Ryker turned to Mia. The lights of the city shimmered in the window. Her blond hair gleamed in the sparkle of night light, and her skin looked so soft and touchable. She stood very still, waiting.

In that moment, Ryker fell even more in love with her. She was his heart, his life. He stepped closer then pulled her into his arms. "You tempt me beyond all limits."

"Who says you have to resist?" Mia whispered, then raked her fingers through his hair.

Ryker scooped her into his arms and carried her to the bedroom. She felt so good against his chest, so loving and feminine. He'd planned to take it nice and slow, as he had a few times before. But Mia wrapped her hands behind his neck and leaned into him.

The passion in her kiss unleashed Ryker's need. He wanted her so bad it hurt. Like a teenager, he frantically stripped her clothes off, craving her nakedness. And Mia responded in kind by peeling off his shirt and yanking down his pants.

All the while, Ryker kissed her, separating only long enough to discard another garment. Then he lifted Mia up to his waist, and she wrapped her legs around him. He kissed her bare skin and flicked his tongue over her nipples until she whimpered.

Then Ryker placed her against the pillows. Mia fisted his cock until he nearly came unglued. She used both hands, using light pressure, then harder. Her ministrations became more intense. She sucked and licked, pushing his arousal to an uncontrollable level.

Taking charge, Ryker pushed her onto the mattress, holding her wrists. Then he kissed down her body until his face was between her legs. He tasted her sweet juices then licked and teased.

Mia squirmed and moaned. "Ryker…please…I need you."

When Ryker spread her legs wider, Mia arched her back. As sexy as it was for her to beg, he couldn't hold out much longer. Quickly, he reached in the side drawer for a condom. He kissed Mia deeply then dipped inside her.

Mia's warmth surrounded him, making his swollen cock ache. He plunged deep, and Mia rocked up to meet him. He stroked into her, and she matched his rhythm. The pleasure took hold and he increased his pace.

Ryker couldn't be close enough, or deep enough. He wanted Mia with his heart and soul. When she cried out and held on tight, he took joy from her climax. And while she was still at her peak, Ryker let go and released inside her.

She held on to Ryker, and he opened his heart. The ecstasy carried him to new heights; he was one with her. He rolled onto his back, pulling Mia on top of him. She sighed and kissed his neck. Satisfaction engulfed him and love possessed him.

*****

The next morning, Ryker snuggled with Mia until the last minute. Then he let her shower while he made breakfast. He made coffee then eggs and toast. Mia came out looking like a fashion model in a business suit. She seemed to glow from the inside.

Mia stood behind him with her arms around his waist. "How is it that you look as sexy in the morning cooking up eggs as you did in bed?"

Ryker turned in her arms and tipped her chin

up for a kiss. "Don't get me started, or you'll be right back in bed."

"Tease." Mia got a mug and poured her coffee.

Ryker served breakfast then sat across from her. His admiration for her went way beyond the bedroom. She was an amazing woman, and he was a lucky guy.

"Are you staring?" Mia said, shuffling eggs onto her fork.

"Yes…I'm staring."

"You're going to make me blush," Mia said.

"If I haven't done that yet, then I need to work on my skills."

"I'll be glad to help you with that."

Ryker put his hand over hers. "I'm sure you would."

The night had been theirs, but reality waited outside the door. "I have to get security for your event finalized today. While you're at the office, Caleb will be on duty."

"You do know how to build a woman up, just to let her down."

"I'll be there to pick you up for dinner," Ryker said.

"I suppose I'll settle for that."

Ryker guessed that life would get rockier for Mia before it smoothed out. He wished he could prevent that. Handling security was his duty, that was one thing he could do for Mia.

While Mia finished breakfast, Ryker showered and dressed. It didn't take long, then he was back to escort her to the parking lot, where Caleb was waiting.

At the door, Mia paused, so Ryker gave her one more tender kiss. He leaned away then mouthed, "I love you."

Tears glistened in Mia's eyes. "You're going to make me ruin my makeup." Then she kissed him again before leaving to face the day.

*****

At Black Swan, Ryker refocused. It was time to tend to business. Mia had stolen his heart, along with the hearts of her adoring public. She was highly visible in the tech world, but her fame extended beyond her accomplishments. Her eye for fashion and her rapport with her supporters made her more than a business owner.

If the media could be believed, fans thought of her as a friend. Mia was a female CEO and the creator of impressive software. Her accomplishments deserved to be acknowledged. Yet Ryker knew he was dealing with more than that.

Fans bonded with Mia and wanted to know more about her and her personal life. That need had been satisfied recently in social media, with positive and negative news. Due to the scandal of the lawsuit followed by private photos, things had gotten out of control.

The media had gone crazy with the story. Speculation was shared, even when based on false assumptions. It seemed everyone had an opinion, and all the conversation had put Mia at the top of their minds.

As flattering as such attention was, it was also dangerous. Fans were excitable and could be unpredictable. The imagined friendship transcended boundaries, causing fans to expect more personal contact. It was a tricky balance between relating to fans and keeping it professional.

The tech event was high-profile. It was a major event with various sectors represented. The presentations, parties, and meetings went on for a week. Mia was part of the development conference and was scheduled to give a presentation.

Each conference was held at a separate location around the downtown area. Although security would be most important at Mia's conference, the team had done reconnaissance at all the locations. It was best to know how it was all planned out.

Setup had been ongoing, but the final preparations had to be completed. Mia's conference was tomorrow. Ryker went to see Amanda and found her at the computer. She finished what she was typing then looked up.

Ryker sat down then went over a few details. "I think we're pretty well set."

"Yes, I'll be at the event under the guise of being Mia's personal assistant. Jake will appear to be event personnel." Amanda smiled. "You'll go as the boyfriend, of course."

"Yeah, very clever of you to think of *that*."

"Hey, smart aleck, it fits right in," Amanda said. "We aren't obvious but can go undercover. You kind of blew your cover when you got your face plastered all over social media with Mia."

"All right, your point is made," Ryker said. "And Lonnie is confirmed?"

"Yep, he requested the duty, so he will be in charge of law enforcement at the conference." Amanda looked at a list she most likely had memorized. "And Hawke will be in the audience as an attendee. I told him to find something businesslike to wear."

"Have we missed anything?"

Amanda looked at him, as if thinking that over. "I hope not."

Ryker went to the lunchroom for coffee. He sat at an empty table. The event should go off without a hitch. Security was tight, but public venues were difficult to manage. There were too many variables.

It didn't make him feel any better that James

was on the list of attendees. Ryker had made it a priority to learn more about stalkers. He'd learned that over half of domestic violence homicides occurred at the point of separation—or after the victim had already left the abuser.

He hadn't shared that revelation with Mia, as it would only scare her. It was his job to make sure she wasn't one of those statistics. It didn't have to get to that point, anyway. The team had been watching James, ensuring that he didn't get close to her.

Amanda stood in the doorway.

"Is there something else?" Ryker said.

"I just received some information I've been waiting for." Amanda sat across from him. "I want to tell you before anyone else."

"What is it?"

"James has a record."

"I thought you ran a background check and told me he didn't have one," Ryker said.

"He doesn't have one that's publicly accessible," Amanda said. "There's a law in this state that allows for certain records to be sealed. It is as though the criminal record never existed."

"How do you know about it, then?"

Amanda rolled her eyes. "I said *publicly* accessible. I have my connections, and it turns out that James was charged with assault. The victim was a woman. But he wasn't convicted, and that's one of the conditions upon which an attorney can base the request to wipe the record clean."

Ryker tried to wrap his head around this new information. "I've seen the guy in action. In a courtroom, I can see a judge believing him, taking his side. He's a good bullshitter."

"And it's not the only time he got away with it," Amanda said. "He has a juvenile record, too. But those records are automatically closed when the person turns eighteen."

"Assault?"

"Yes, and also a female victim."

Ryker's blood turned cold. "And that's just the two incidents we know about." He considered sharing this new information with Mia, but there was no point. The event would be stressful enough without giving her more reason for concern. "It's our job to make sure that Mia isn't added to his list of victims."

CHAPTER 16

On the morning of the event, Mia dressed in her new outfit. She spent extra time on her hair and put on more makeup for the cameras. She'd only had toast and coffee for breakfast, since she was too nervous to have much appetite.

She drew strength from knowing that Ryker would be with her for support and the team would be there to protect her. It was a big event and would be filmed. The current situation was volatile, yet she hoped to calm the public with her talk.

Mental Magic hung in a delicate balance. On stage, she would be speaking to nervous investors, overly excited fans, and concerned parents. Plus, her own team was counting on her. The weighty burden of inspiring confidence rested on her shoulders.

When Mia was as ready as she could be, she went out to find Ryker already dressed. He wore a navy blazer and light blue shirt with charcoal slacks. When he smiled at her, it made her heart skip a beat. He was so handsome. Her protector had morphed into a corporate heartthrob.

"You'll have the audience swooning for you," Mia said. "No one will be listening to me at all."

"I didn't know the business look was sexy. I'll have to buy more blazers."

Mia's phone rang. It was Griffen, so she answered. "Calling to wish me luck?" She motioned to Ryker that she'd be a minute, then sat down.

"I have news for you, and I wanted to deliver it before the event," Griffen said. "I think it will give you some peace of mind."

"I'm all ears."

Griffen proceeded to relay the news he'd received from the attorney that very morning. Mia listened then relief washed over her. "I'm so glad you called. Finally, something goes in our favor."

When the call ended, Mia looked at Ryker.

"Good news?"

"Yes, it was," Mia said. "I was a little stunned, so I'm not sure if I got all of what Griffen told me. But the drift of it is that the lawsuit has been dismissed."

"That's a better outcome than you'd hoped."

"Our attorney filed for dismissal because the claim had no basis in law or fact," Mia said. "The court considered it a frivolous lawsuit."

"How do they determine that?"

"The attorney said that it's a lawsuit filed with the intention of harassing, annoying, or disturbing the opposite party."

"That's a yes on all three," Ryker said.

"And the court stated that James knew there was little chance of succeeding if he pursued the case in court," Mia said. "That's good news and bad."

Ryker raised his brows.

"It's too late for a reversal of the divorce," Mia said. "Now, the lawsuit has been thrown out. James doesn't handle failure well. He's used to having things go his way."

"He'll react to control being taken from him," Ryker said. "He maneuvered to gain the upper hand, his attempt to force your obedience." He paused. "I don't like this at all. It could make him snap."

"It would serve him right," Mia said. "He's been my oppressor for far too long. He needs to learn that those days are over."

Ryker stood in front of Mia and put his hands on her shoulders. His expression was serious, and Mia wondered what was wrong.

"I won't allow you to go to the event," Ryker said. "Not today. I won't let you risk it. It's not safe."

Mia was aware that James would know about the lawsuit before the event started. And he would be pissed. But she had to go anyway.

"You're still so bossy!" Mia pulled away. "You can't tell me what to do. I refuse to cower or hide." She glared at Ryker. "My entire life hasn't been *safe*. Why should today be any different?"

Mia stormed out, with Ryker following her to the car. She was mad and sick to death of being ordered about. She got in the car without another word.

Ryker drove and Mia fumed. Yet she sensed there was more that Ryker hadn't told her. She didn't know what had caused him to have a change of heart. It couldn't be the lawsuit; that was only part of it. Just days before, Ryker had been supportive. He'd told her not to worry, that he'd protect her.

Mia was frustrated. There was something Ryker wasn't sharing. She knew him too well and could see it in his expression. She had no idea what it could be. And why didn't he tell her? Did he have so little faith in her?

*****

Mia arrived early while the setup was still in progress. Ryker introduced her to Amanda, her new assistant, then went off to coordinate the team. There was a small office where they could talk and get to know each other. They had to appear as though they worked together.

Amanda wore a business suit and looked very

fit. She had bright red hair twisted into a professional style and wore expertly applied eye shadow to accent her blue eyes.

"It's good to meet you," Mia said. "Ryker tells me that you were in the Air Force."

"Yes, I worked in communications," Amanda said. "That's deceiving, though. We had to be as fit as anyone else."

"I'm sure." Mia could tell that Amanda wasn't up for idle chitchat, which she appreciated.

"I know what it's like to be a woman in a man's world," Amanda said, then proceeded to share a few incidents to make her point. It seemed that she'd stood up to the pressure quite well.

"It appears we have a lot in common," Mia said. "I admire your spunk."

"I understand male aggression. I don't put up with it. And I understand what you have to deal with, regarding James in particular."

"I have a feeling you understand better than most."

"I'm trained to protect you," Amanda said. "Since I'm a woman, I can stay close to you without alarm bells going off."

"I'm more relaxed knowing that you'll be with me at the podium."

"I don't trust the situation. It's too public and you're too vulnerable," Amanda said. "I know that Ryker taught you some self-defense moves."

"Yes, we worked on the ones he thought were vital."

"I have another one for you," Amanda said. "It's a move for women, one that I'm guessing he didn't teach you."

Amanda demonstrated how to escape from a bear-hug attack. Then she let Mia try. The setup was an attacker coming from behind. The purpose of the move was to create space and get free.

"Bend from the waist," Amanda said. "That shifts your weight forward, making it more difficult for your attacker to pick you up. It gives you a better angle to throw your elbows from side to side, hitting his face."

It was an effective move, and Mia got the hang of it quickly. Once she had loosened the attacker's hold, she could use elbow jabs like Ryker had taught her, then other tactics to injure the attacker's face or groin, making escape possible.

"That's a move to remember," Amanda said. "A man tends to come from behind then wrap his arms around you—on the assumption that he is stronger than you."

Mia ran through the moves once more, then she had it.

"And if attacked, be loud and threatening," Amanda said. "An attacker expects you to be afraid and intimidated, but will hesitate if you're attracting attention or appear to be more of a challenge than anticipated."

"I'll remember that," Mia said. "Are you expecting trouble today?"

Amanda smiled. "I'm always expecting trouble. It's all about how prepared you are." She motioned toward the door. "Ready?"

Mia went out to get ready for her talk. Iris found her and came over to offer support. "You'll do great. I have complete confidence in you," she said, then gave Mia a hug.

Griffen had taken a seat near the front. He nodded at Mia then smiled. It was good to have friends in the audience.

A few rows back, Hawke sat next to a couple of women. He looked muscular, even with a jacket on. But he'd worn business attire and maintained an appropriate attitude. Mia wasn't supposed to acknowledge that she knew him, as his presence was more discreet that way.

Law enforcement was stationed at the entrance, screening attendees. And Jake was in the aisle directing them to open seats. Amanda had pointed him out, so Mia knew he was on the team.

Mia made her way to the front then sat beside Ryker. He looked over but didn't say anything. He was taking in the scene, while appearing semi-bored. He called it situational awareness.

The presentation was coming up, so Mia's

thoughts were on that. The development conference was about problem solving and innovative solutions. It occurred to Mia that was precisely what she could use in her personal life.

Ryker's knee touched hers, drawing her attention to his presence. She was still annoyed with him. On reflection, it was less because of him trying to tell her what to do, and more about him keeping something from her.

Before Mia had a chance to ponder that further, Ryker's phone vibrated. It was a text from Hawke. He replied then said, "It seems some tweet this morning caused a sensation and the fans are going wild."

Mia guessed it was probably about Ryker being her boyfriend. Sometimes she felt more like a movie star than a company CEO, the way her life was held up to scrutiny. Tweeting about her love life would be a slap in the face to James. His ego wouldn't be able to take much more.

"When you go up there to speak," Ryker said, "Jake will be near the stage...just in case."

The presentations began and Mia watched, only half listening. There had been no sign of James. Maybe he wouldn't show up after all.

Just before lunch, Mia was announced. She made her way to the podium, nervous but determined. Amanda accompanied her to handle the slides and fulfill her role as assistant. Once

Mia was in front of the group delivering her well-rehearsed speech, she got into a rhythm. She was motivated and inspired.

Mia talked about raising the level of competence of youth and revolutionizing the educational system. The Mental Magic software was meant to enable learning and could even make it easier for companies to train employees.

The first goal was to make it available to students with a learning disability. Her company's purpose was to give kids a chance in a tough world. The presentation appeared well received. There was applause at a couple of points, which encouraged Mia to continue.

Before Mia's talk was over, James arrived. She couldn't help but see him, since he managed to find a seat near the front—likely to antagonize her. With a glance, she saw that he'd worn a designer suit and that he appeared cool and calm. It was unnerving.

James took a seat, and Mia tried to block out the attention he focused on her, refusing to look at him. Then she noticed that Eddie was with him. Chills ran up her spine. Why did James bring his nephew? He didn't even like the boy.

CHAPTER 17

Ryker listened to Mia's talk and was proud of her. The audience was responding well, laughing and applauding at appropriate points. The team was in place, and there was no visible sign of a threat—but Ryker watched and waited.

Late in the presentation, James arrived and took a seat in one of the front rows. But there was no sign of aggression, and he would have been screened at the door for weapons. Was it possible that Mia's ex realized that it was over? It was out of character to admit failure. At some point, James had to see that things weren't going to happen like he wanted.

James had his nephew with him, the eight-year old kid Mia had been tutoring. But that didn't add up. James had disowned the boy, and now he was playing the role of favorite uncle? It was puzzling. The speech ended, and the crowd took a lunch break in another room.

Amanda looked down from the stage and caught Ryker's eye. He nodded. They were in sync, each knowing their function. Amanda followed Mia down the steps then over to Ryker. He congratulated her and gave her a hug, not wanting to let her go. If only he could whisk her away, out of public reach.

Mia seemed pleased with how she'd delivered her speech. She grabbed her purse from the chair and put the strap over her shoulder. She appeared more relaxed than she had been that morning. On the way to lunch, Mia chatted about how she'd felt on stage and her relief that it was over.

The lunchroom was a large room with many round tables covered in white tablecloths. It had a cork ceiling and carpeted floors with side doors for the waitstaff. It was an enclosed environment and seemed safe enough.

Ryker motioned toward James, who was across the room, and Jake acknowledged with a nod. His teammate would keep an eye on the one threat in the room to be sure he was only there to have lunch.

On the way to the table, attendees came up to Mia to greet her and express excitement about the new software. It was a positive sign, and Mia was cordial to each person who talked to her. Ryker ushered her to a seat at the table.

Before Mia sat down, James came over to congratulate her. Ryker bristled at the gall he had to approach the table.

"Might I say that I was quite impressed,"

James said. "I apologize for being late, but I had to pick up Eddie. He didn't want to miss your big day."

Mia handled it well and showed no signs of animosity. She was too smart to antagonize James. The goal was to make it through the event without incident. "That's kind of you to say, James. I'm glad you enjoyed my talk."

Eddie stepped forward, so Mia bent down to hug him. He was a quiet boy with dark hair and big eyes. She appeared very fond of him.

"Are we going to play more games this summer?" Eddie said.

Mia smiled. "I'm planning on it. And you look so nice all dressed up. I didn't know you'd be here today, but I hope you're having a good time."

James took Eddie's hand to guide him to another table, where other attendees were already seated. Ryker watched him go, then looked at Hawke, who was at a table in between Mia and James. Hawke acted as though he was unaware that anything had transpired, but Ryker was sure he didn't miss a thing.

All seemed well. Law enforcement was still at the entrance. Amanda sat on one side of Mia, and Ryker sat on the other with a clear view of James. Lunch service was prompt. The food was the usual fare of steak or chicken with some side dishes.

During the meal, Mia talked to Iris and Griffen from across the table. She shared some highlights of her experience at the podium and what she'd noticed about the audience. The mood was very celebratory, making Ryker wonder if was too soon for that. He was still on protection duty, so wouldn't relax until Mia was out of there.

*****

Under the table, Mia held Ryker's hand. She couldn't recall what she'd been angry about. Whatever it was didn't matter anymore. The presentation had gone well, so she was much calmer. It was nice to eat lunch and share the experience with her team.

The only annoyance had been James. His presence had ruined an otherwise smooth presentation. His arrival had given Mia pause, and she'd lagged in her talk. But she'd resumed gracefully, so doubted that the audience had noticed.

It was nice to see Eddie, and she was glad it looked promising for him now. Over the summer, he had a good chance of catching up on his studies—if the board came through with the approval. She'd done her best to sway public sentiment and was sure the board was in tune with such things.

James irked her. He was as slick as ever with his polished manners and impeccable attire. It struck her that he behaved like a man who had won. That made her wonder if he'd finally seen that it was over, and that the danger had passed.

When the meal ended, attendees began to filter out. Iris and Griffen headed back to their seats in the auditorium. "I'll see you in there," Iris said.

Mia hung back, as someone stopped to offer her encouragement. She appreciated the support and made that known.

When the room was nearly empty, Mia put her purse strap over her shoulder and linked her arm with Ryker's. He held her to his side, and it felt good. Amanda stood to her left, looking like the willing assistant.

Then Eddie rushed over and hugged Mia around the waist. James wasn't far behind.

"Mia...I have so much more fun with you," Eddie said.

James seemed overly focused on Mia, making her feel like a target. His attention aroused her curiosity, so she looked up and their eyes met. Then James reached for Eddie. She wondered if he intended to take his nephew home or make him sit through an afternoon of boring speeches—for surely a child wouldn't be interested in the presentations.

In a flash, James grabbed Eddie. He pulled a steak knife from his jacket pocket and held it to the kid's throat, causing him to shriek. Mia was shocked, and her protection team froze.

Ryker didn't move a muscle, and Amanda stood at attention. Hawke looked like an apparition standing off to the side.

"You're hurting me, Uncle James."

"Shut up!" James jerked the knife, and a drop of blood rolled down Eddie's neck. The boy was crying.

"Don't do this," Mia said.

"Let the kid go." Ryker sounded calm and in control.

Mia struggled to understand what was happening, then saw Amanda stare at James. She was likely wondering the same thing: what did James have in mind?

"James," Amanda said, speaking slowly and in a deep voice. She sounded like a late-night radio DJ, and the attention went to her. "You don't want to do this. Consider the consequences; you're a respected man. But if you harm your nephew...you won't be able to undo that."

James emitted a guttural laugh, then refocused on Mia.

"Let him go," Hawke said, taking a step closer. "If you do, no one will press charges."

As if he hadn't heard, James said, "Here's how it's going to go." He stared at Mia. "You will come with me or I'll kill the kid."

Silence followed, as no one seemed to know

how to react, least of all Mia.

"You know I mean it," James said. "You haven't forgotten I'll use force when necessary."

Mia's heart fell. She could see no way out. Eddie was crying now. "It's okay," she said. "Your uncle is kidding around. You'll be all right."

Then James snapped; it was frightening to see his fury unleashed. "You have two seconds to agree to come with me, or I'll slice the kid's neck."

Eddie sobbed, and his small body shook. James held the knife firmly at his jugular. One wrong move and the boy would be dead. Mia panicked. "I'll go. Calm down. I'll do what you ask. Just let Eddie go."

"You think I'm that stupid?" James said, his eyes dark. "You have a small army here that will grab me the instant I take this knife away. Eddie goes with us. No one is to follow." He looked at Amanda. "Your assistant can come along. Once I'm sure we're safe, I'll release Eddie and she can bring him back."

Cautiously, Mia moved forward to walk beside James. He lifted Eddie in his arms to increase the pace of their departure. He held the knife at his throat. Amanda followed, but the others stayed back. At the rear of the building, there was an exit that led to the alley.

James motioned toward the door, so Mia opened it to step out. A black sedan with darkened windows pulled up. When the door opened, she saw a heavyset male in the back seat. She glanced to the front seat, taking note that the driver was a muscular guy with dark glasses.

Before getting in the car, James asked for their cell phones. "I wouldn't want anyone tracking us." He took both phones and tossed them down the alley.

James motioned for Amanda to get in, then Mia followed. After James got in the front passenger seat with Eddie, the doors locked. Mia's heart was breaking. She couldn't see Eddie but heard him sobbing. He must be so scared.

The car pulled away and sped off. Mia was glad that Amanda was with her, but she wouldn't be for long. The two thugs aiding James looked familiar. Then Mia remembered the two from the night she'd been robbed and had to lock herself in the bathroom.

The masks they'd worn hadn't disguised their size or general bearing. The likeness was too strong; she was sure they were the same men. The two spoke a Baltic language as they had that night. She'd thought that James had been behind that robbery, and now she knew for sure. He'd been more of a threat than she'd realized.

Amanda gave James a scathing look, with such fire in her eyes that Mia thought he might incinerate on the spot. Yet that was only wishful thinking. It would take more than that to get them all out of trouble.

Mia struggled to come up with some tactic that would change the odds, but nothing came to mind. She couldn't risk any sudden moves with a knife at Eddie's throat. Amanda caught her eye and gave a slight nod toward the driver. Mia saw that he had a gun strap. The men were armed.

Whatever Mia did, she'd have to wait until Eddie was safe. She prayed that James would let the boy go. If only she could see Eddie's face to give him a look of reassurance. But she was helpless in the back seat.

The driver took a route through the city, but Mia couldn't tell where he was headed. He kept looking in the rearview to be sure no one followed. Then he made various turns to change the route, which made the trip more confusing.

The longer and more circuitous the trip was, the more anxious Mia became. "When are you going to let Eddie go? You promised. I'll only cooperate if you keep your word." She didn't know how much the word of a psycho was worth.

"I'll release him," James said. "If I have to listen to this kid whine much longer, I *will* kill him. But I don't need a murder charge to deal with. That would ruin everything."

On the edge of town, in an area that Mia wasn't familiar with, the driver finally pulled off. James opened the door, holding Eddie with the knife still at his throat.

"You're okay, Eddie," Mia said. "Amanda has you. Your mommy is waiting for you. I'll be fine. Don't worry."

"Oh, don't make me sick," James said, then looked at Amanda. "Get out."

Mia opened the door and stood on the sidewalk, so Amanda could slide out.

"Move back," James said, and Amanda complied. "Farther back." When she was far enough up the block, he told Mia to get in the back seat. Then he sat beside her still holding Eddie. It looked for a moment as though he was going to take the boy.

Then the driver hit the gas and James tossed Eddie to the street before slamming the door shut. Mia saw Amanda sprinting toward the boy. The car sped away then turned at the first corner. Mia was lodged between James and his accomplice. She was alone, so would have to fend for herself.

The self-defense moves she'd learned seemed useless. She wasn't prepared to handle men with guns. Mia had underestimated James. "What do you hope to gain?" she said. "I won't stay with you."

Mia wondered if James planned to kill her. But if so, why not do it now? Maybe he wanted to get out of the city first. Terror gripped her; he could murder her and dispose of her body so no one would know.

"Oh, I think you'll stay with me," James said. "You're *mine*. I thought you'd realized that by now."

CHAPTER 18

Ryker's heart ripped in half. Mia was gone. He had to get her back. His training kicked in and he blocked out the emotion. It took all his inner strength but was the only way. Then he went into action.

He'd trained for this; he could save her. There had been no way to stop James from taking Mia without risking Eddie's life. Ryker had stood mute while his love was swept out of the building. He had given Mia a look to let her know he would follow, but he was unsure if she noticed.

Hawke went to the entrance to alert Lonnie, so law enforcement could handle the public. The event would be ended.

Jake had slipped out and gone around the building to see what he could, then returned with information. "James went out the back to a car in the alley. I got the make and model but couldn't see inside. The windows were too dark."

"Did you get the plate?" Ryker said.

"No rear plate."

Ryker would inform Lonnie, so an alert could be sent out to watch for the car. But without a plate, it was fairly pointless. "I have to find her, try to follow. It's the only option right now."

"I'll stay here and text if I find out anything useful," Jake said.

Ryker went to his car and headed for the main downtown streets. It seemed futile, but he felt like he was doing something. Maybe he'd get lucky. But Philly was a big city with too many places to go. It was like trying to find a needle in a haystack. And he had to be careful, because if he did find the car, he had to make sure the driver wasn't aware of being followed.

After forty minutes of driving around, Ryker pulled into a parking lot to decide what was next. There had to be a better way. He vaguely hoped the police would be useful, that the car would be spotted. Then his phone rang, but he didn't recognize the number.

"Ryker...it's Amanda. I'm out of the car."

"What phone are you calling from?"

"I borrowed some guy's cell," Amanda said. "Eddie is okay. I have him. He has some scrapes and is scared to death. I'll get him to his mother."

"Where's Mia?"

"She's with James, and there are two other guys in the car," Amanda said. "It looks like he hired some muscle."

"Where are they headed? Could you tell?"

"Jake can tell you," Amanda said. "Have him

log in to the feed. I put a tracker in Mia's purse."

"When did you do that?"

"Dude...what do you think, this is amateur hour?" Amanda said. "I slipped it in her purse when I was with her in the office. It's a global tracker about the size of a dime. The battery lasts two weeks, but I don't think Mia has that long, unless you get to her."

"Glad you were thinking ahead."

"The purse is the best place," Amanda said. "I didn't want to chance putting it on her body. If it gets physical, James could find it."

Rage unfurled in Ryker's belly. The thought of James getting physical with Mia, sexual or otherwise, made him want to smash the guy into the concrete.

"I'll take a cab back and have Lonnie contact Eddie's mother," Amanda said. "I'll see you when I see you."

Ryker called Jake and had him log in to the system.

"Yes, I see it," Jake said. "The feed is coming through."

"Can you tell where the car is headed?"

"Give me a second. Let me check the map."

Ryker waited impatiently. He pulled out onto the street, ready to go after the car.

"The car is headed for the airport," Jake said. "I'm watching the movement and it is the most logical destination. There's no other reason to take the freeway toward that exit."

"Access the flight data, then alert Lonnie, so he can stop them from boarding," Ryker said. "James can be arrested before takeoff."

"Getting flight data may take some time. I hope they are using real names," Jake said. "And the tracker has a limited radius. I can tell you when she's near the airport, but I can't lead you to her specific location. It's not as precise as the military model."

Ryker ended the call to get the airport. He knew the city, so took the fastest route. He only hoped to get there in time. The cops might not act quickly enough, so he'd have to prevent the plane from taking off.

He loved Mia with all his heart. He wouldn't let harm come to her. James wanted Mia for himself, so wouldn't kill her unless provoked, which was an advantage. It would buy some time, but how much?

Ryker arrived at the airport then jogged to the main terminal. He'd just entered when Jake called.

"Talk to me," Ryker said.

"I got what you asked," Jake said, "but it's not helpful. There are no passengers on any airlines named Mia Scott or James Walsh. I'll keep looking to see what I can come up with."

"I'm here," Ryker said. "I'll look around and see if I can spot them." He was at the entrance, but it was mobbed with travelers. Philadelphia International was huge.

To better the odds, Ryker asked around. He went up to other passengers to politely inquire if they'd seen Mia Scott, a name many recognized. He gave a story that they'd had an argument, and she'd left. He didn't know her flight. After describing her, he hoped that someone had seen her.

Ryker had no success. There were too many people, and even a well-known face like Mia's went unnoticed. A couple of times, he spotted a woman who looked like Mia and his heart skipped a beat. But it wasn't her. Desperation began to take over, but Ryker tried to keep cool.

It was taking too long. They had to be there somewhere. How hard could it be to find two people escorted by a couple of thugs?

Then Jake called. "I found it. It's a private jet. The pilot filed a flight plan. I accessed the computers, and his passengers are James Walsh and guests."

"Where are they going?"

"The plane is flying to Spain," Jake said.

"I have to stop them!"

"You can't," Jake said. "The plane already took off. But Hawke is arranging a jet to go after them.

I'll bring all we need. Caleb is on his way with your passport from headquarters."

"Bring it to me, and I'll take it from there," Ryker said. "I can handle the two protection guys, and James will be easy pickings after that."

"I'm going with you," Jake said. "You need me to handle the tracking. And I speak Spanish."

"Okay, tell Hawke to hustle with that jet."

*****

Mia was on a private jet, sitting beside James. The guards were in seats across the aisle. It was a nightmare. He was taking her out of the city. That was bad news. Mia had looked into Ryker's eyes before leaving, so had faith that he would try to follow. But how could he find her, if she was in a remote location?

"Where are we going?" Mia said.

"To Europe," James said. "You wanted to travel, so now you have the opportunity."

Mia freaked out. How in the hell was she supposed to deal with Europe? What if she didn't speak the language? She'd have to get free of her captors then get home.

"Where in Europe?"

"You'll see," James said, and he seemed unwilling to offer more.

The accommodations would have been nice if it wasn't for the circumstances. Mia was a prisoner. She ate and drank very little. After a long time, she put the seat back to try to rest but was too anxious. The flight was long and getting longer. She just wanted it to be over.

After what seemed like forever, the plane landed. Mia had lost track of time, but it must have been over eight hours. She didn't have a way to check and was disoriented. When she exited the plane, the guards walked beside her.

Mia bided her time, waiting for a chance to escape, but no opportunity arose. Once inside the airport, she realized the plane had landed in Barcelona. It had been a long trip and she was frazzled.

It was important to stay alert. Mia remembered Ryker telling her about combat duty and how vital it was to stay in control. She tried to interact with James, but he was tight-lipped. She found out very little. The guards escorted them to a car then headed away from the airport.

Mia hoped that the destination wasn't far, but that wasn't the case. Due to the time difference, it was already afternoon in Spain, and she was thankful for daylight. The drive was several hours, but James refused to tell her exactly where they were going. The country was lovely, with high mountain peaks all around, and the weather was pleasant.

A large river flowed by the road, and Mia wished she knew more about the country. The road went through a valley, and the car stopped at a border crossing into a country called Andorra. The guard in the front passenger seat gave her a menacing look and flashed his gun to remind her to keep quiet.

Mia tried to subdue her panic. Crossing into another country wasn't promising. It would be another barrier to getting home. But there wasn't much she could do but wait. James showed their passports at the crossing.

Either James had stolen hers or had another made, which wouldn't have been too difficult, considering that she was still married to him. She watched as they drove through a big city. A sign said it was Andorra la Vella, the capital. She hadn't heard of the place before.

The highway beyond the border cut through the mountains, and the elevation got higher as they went. There were homes dotted on the hillsides along the way and snow covered the high peaks. There were more rocky cliffs than trees. And the higher the road went, the scarier it was, as the low guard rails didn't provide much of a barrier against plummeting to the depths below.

It was depressing that Mia's first trip to Europe was with a man she despised. The mountainous trip might have been an adventure instead of a frightening trek up a narrow, curvy road. She was in the Spanish section of the

Pyrenees; she knew that much about geography. There were majestic views all around, yet she took little pleasure in the sight.

During the trip, James was silent. And she didn't think she'd heard the guards utter more than a couple of words. Mia would have to see where they were taking her. As it was, she couldn't leap from a speeding car. Plus, there were steep cliffs on both sides. The car continued up the steep mountains, carrying her farther from safety with each mile.

*****

Ryker and Jake arrived at the Barcelona airport prepared to rescue Mia. The jet landed hours after Mia's, since it had taken a while for Hawke to arrange things. But it had happened as fast as possible. It was early evening by the time they disembarked.

The pilot would wait for a text to let him know they were ready to return. Ryker hoped that would be fairly soon, although he didn't know how far James had taken Mia. A car with snow tires was waiting for them, thanks to Hawke.

Ryker drove while Jake monitored the feed from the tracker on his phone. He guided their way, as he was able to see where the tracker was and could navigate with a map from there. Unfortunately, due to the delay, James had a head start and was quite a distance from the airport.

It was torture to drive through Spain, tediously making his way to Mia. Ryker wanted to speed it up, worried about what James might do.

"We'll get there as quick as we can," Jake said, as if reading his buddy's mind. "Her captor's state of mind is an issue. There's no telling what could happen."

"Possession of Mia should be a salve to James's ego," Ryker said. "That may repress his violent nature for a while."

"Let's just hope that it's long enough."

After hours of travel, Jake said, "It looks like they're crossing into Andorra."

"Where is that? I've never heard of it."

"It's a small country between Spain and France," Jake said. "When I was a boy, I lived in Spain with my family for many years. That's how I learned to speak Spanish."

"Why is James taking her there?"

"There are advantages," Jake said. "For one, the country has no extradition treaty with the U.S. It's also a wealthy country and a nice place to live. It's in the Pyrenees."

"This could get interesting."

"Yep, I think so," Jake said. "I'm familiar with the area, as I visited the country a few times. It's an easy trip across the border. Actually, it's a clever choice, a good place to hide out."

"James is insane, but he's not stupid."

There was no hold-up at the border crossing. Soon Ryker was driving on a mountain road. The tracker led them closer to Mia and her captors. At one point, Jake said, "Their car has arrived. The tracker shows they are in a stable location."

Ryker drove a winding, narrow road. Up ahead were steep mountains and rough terrain. He reached a point where he could leave the car. It was best to go the rest of the way on foot. Jake followed him up the trail until they came to a residence.

Farther up was a chalet lit with small outdoor lights. Snow covered the high peaks surrounding the location. It was on the side of a mountain with no other residences around. Ryker and Jake scouted the area, quiet as cats. The structure was a two-story building with an upper-level terrace.

A period of surveillance revealed that there were two guards. There was no evidence of any backup. The guards were posted on the perimeter, which left Mia inside with James. The shutters were closed, so it was impossible to see inside. But darkness would work to Ryker and Jake's advantage, making it difficult for the enemy to see their approach.

Ryker would prefer to know what they were walking into. He didn't want to take a chance with Mia's safety. But every minute of delay increased the risk of Mia getting hurt. Ryker didn't have the luxury of staking out the place for days.

Their plan was to knock the guards unconscious with a blow to the cranium, then get inside and rescue Mia. Once James was alone, taking him into custody shouldn't be a problem. The place didn't have any special security. The lock would be easy for Jake to pick. The challenge was to maintain silence. It was important that James wasn't aware that anything was happening until it was too late.

CHAPTER 19

James had taken Mia to a chalet in the mountains. She hadn't seen any other residents around, so her hope of getting help evaporated. So much for being loud and intimidating; there was no one close enough to hear her.

Upon arrival, James ushered her inside. The other two stood guard outside, and Mia looked around. There was a stone fireplace, hardwood floors, and thick area rugs. It looked like a vacation getaway. The window on one wall was wide and ran from floor to ceiling, offering a picturesque view.

Mia walked over and parted the curtains of the upper-story window. It had a narrow ledge with a low railing, with enough space to set flowerpots. The chalet was perched on the side of a mountain. Outside there was a steep cliff, and she peered down, feeling a bit dizzy.

The scene in the distance was beautiful, with snow on the mountaintops and craggy cliffs all around. But the terrain was treacherous. If she escaped, she'd have make it down the narrow mountain road.

Mia tried not to think of that just yet. To the side of the window was a vase filled with flowers. It occurred to her that James had paid to have the place set up for his arrival. The lovely arrangement was supposed to placate her; she knew the methods James used.

Mia turned to look at her captor, who was gloating. "You can't hold me here. I'm a U.S. citizen."

James laughed. "That's the beauty of it. This country has no treaty with the U.S., so there will be no attempt to get you back. There isn't even a consulate here."

Mia was trapped. "How do you plan to support yourself?"

"That shouldn't be a problem. You'll have the money from your business account transferred to a local bank. And if that proves insufficient—which is doubtful—you can write another program. That has been very lucrative."

Mia was incredulous. "What makes you think that I'll cooperate with you?"

"Eddie was only a taste of what I'm capable of," James said. "I don't think you'd want to see anything happen to those you care about."

Mia thought of Iris and Griffen, wondering what exactly he meant.

"You can change clothes," James said. "We'll

have dinner shortly."

Mia stared. He was acting as if he'd taken her on a romantic vacation: the chalet, the flowers, a quiet dinner. It dawned on her just how crazy he was. She went down the hall to find the bedroom. The weather had turned colder high in the mountains.

She hoped there was something warmer to wear and was surprised to find a closet filled with clothes. James knew her size and provided the garments she'd need. After selecting wool pants and a sweater with fur-lined boots, she went to the bathroom and locked the door before dressing.

Ryker had warned her not to go to the event, but Mia hadn't heeded the advice. All of this could have been avoided. But no, the bullying had to stop. She refused to give up; she would find a way to get out of the grip of her abusive ex.

Mia had no idea how to get away. James had made one mistake: if he returned to the U.S., he'd be arrested. But that didn't help much. Mia had to get back to the airport, but how? She'd worry about that later. She had to escape first.

When Mia returned to the living room, James looked her over. "You belong to me, Mia. You want it as much as I do; that's why you fight it so hard."

"You're wrong about that."

"You'll be treated well here," James said, "as long as you behave. You have annoyed me greatly, yet I've been extremely tolerant. You had many chances to come back to me, but you wouldn't listen. Look what that's led to. You have only yourself to blame. You left me no choice."

James stood then walked over. His lascivious look made her cringe. He reached out and touched her cheek, making Mia's skin crawl. "I'm your husband," he said, so close that his breath filled her nostrils.

Mia turned away, then James wrapped his arms around her. She bent over so he couldn't get a tight hold, then twisted and hit his jaw with an elbow strike—just like Amanda had taught her. She twisted the other way to hit again, but James grabbed her arms.

She looked up at James, seeing anger. Yet he seemed to relish the challenge, which was all the worse for her.

"You'll calm down," James said in a chilling tone. "There is nowhere for you to go." He dragged her to kitchen, so she sat at the table.

The table was set with silver and china, along with candles and flowers. The romantic setting looked bizarre. Mia watched as James served her fettuccini and poured wine. Like a predator who had cornered his prey, he began to eat with gusto.

Mia had no appetite but forced herself to eat.

She would need her strength. She hadn't heard the guards for a while. The two were outside to ensure she didn't make a run for it. Meanwhile, James was in a zone, enjoying his meal and appearing confident of his conquest.

That gave Mia a chance to plan. She recalled what Ryker had told her during training. Be willing to harm your attacker, because he surely intends to kill you. Mia had no qualms about taking James out of the picture for good.

When Mia had lived with him, James had beaten her fiercely on more than one occasion. He'd nearly killed her and was back to finish the job. She had to make sure that he didn't succeed. Since Mia had no weapons, she'd have to utilize the defensive moves she'd learned. She'd changed purses before the event, so didn't even have her lipstick taser.

James talked like an insane man. "We are finally together. I'll be nice to you...if you are nice to me."

Mia felt ill. She vowed to end this and get back to Ryker—somehow. The thought of Ryker's love and kindness kept her going; it gave her strength. He wasn't anything like the monster across the table from her.

There were others counting on Mia, and she was determined to come through. She'd been in other scrapes and survived. Even though this was the worst, she swore not to fail. She would get free. There was no way that she'd allow James to conquer her—not without a fight.

When dinner was over, James took her to the other room. He stood by the fire and put his arm around her. Mia pulled away. With hatred in his eyes, James drew back then punched her in the jaw.

Mia was thrown against a chair, but she righted herself. She put her hand to her jaw but didn't think it was broken—although it hurt like hell.

"You insult me," James said. "I've tried to do everything for you, but you disrespect me. Now...come here."

Mia was afraid, but when he got closer, she grabbed on to the chair then kicked her right leg up. She leaned back slightly, then drove her hips forward to thrust her shin up and into his groin. James buckled over but didn't stay incapacitated.

Still folded in half, James reached for the poker from the fireplace and swung it with force. The backhand swing of the iron rod hit her right arm, and she heard a crack. She screamed with pain, but James didn't back off.

Blinded with rage, James staggered toward Mia, so she fled. She raced to the front door and yanked it open with her good arm. Then flew out—right into Ryker's arms. He held on to her, not taking his eyes off James.

Mia turned to see James pointing a pistol at her. He had a smirk on his face. "So, your boyfriend has come to save you. Well, that's not going to happen."

Ryker held Mia close, while she stared into deadly eyes.

"You belong to me," James said, then aimed the pistol. "If I can't have you...no one can."

"Put the gun down," Ryker said. "I'm taking you back to face charges."

James stepped back without lowering the gun. "That's not going to happen."

"You don't want to kill anyone," Ryker said. "Give me the weapon."

James's hand trembled, so he held the gun in both hands. "No!"

In the same instant the gun went off, Ryker spun, so his back was to James and Mia was protected against his chest. He grunted but held tight to her, pressing her head to his chest. She pulled back to see blood on Ryker's side.

A thud at the window made James turn that way. He fired again, and the bullet shattered the glass. Jake leapt through the window, knocking over the vase and spilling the water on the floor. Then he snatched the gun right out of James's hand.

"It's over," Jake said. "Give it up."

But James didn't seem to hear. In a rage, he flew at Jake, who punched him in the gut. James doubled over with a groan but was upright in a flash. He stood with his back to the open window.

Jake approached, holding out his hand. "Let's go. You can't win this."

James growled then raised his right knee and foot for a front kick. He had practiced kickboxing, but Mia hadn't seen him use it before. James extended his leg so the ball of his foot struck Jake's chest. But the impact didn't force Jake off balance.

Instead, it threw James backward, where he teetered at the window with the curtains rustling in the breeze. While Mia watched in horror, James tried to grab the curtain but slipped in the water, as shards of the broken vase crunched under his feet. As if in slow motion, he yelled then fell back and plunged out the window.

Jake made a grab for him, but it was too late.

Mia had her left hand on Ryker's waist and warmth flowed over her fingers. She lifted her hand to see that it was blood. "You were shot."

Ryker grimaced then shrugged. "The wound isn't too bad. I'll bind it up. But your arm is broken."

Only then did Mia feel the excruciating pain in her right arm, hanging limply at her side. She and Ryker were battered but alive. Sheer relief washed over her and tears blurred her vision. "I am so damn glad to see you," she said with a sob.

*****

A few weeks later, Mia was with Ryker at his brother's house. They were visiting on a Sunday, which could easily become routine. Christa was making a casserole, while Ian entertained the kids with a game of tag. Mia could hear the squeals of the children at play.

Ryker's injury had been a flesh wound, so he hadn't spent any time in the hospital. Although he still had a bandage around his middle. That shot had been meant for her, and Mia was sure that she wouldn't have fared as well if it had hit its mark.

Mia's right arm was in a cast, and she looked at the signatures scribbled all over it with fondness. Holding her left hand, Ryker led her out to the kid's swing set, where she took a seat. He took the one next to her and swung in a slow motion.

James had been brought back, so his sister could handle the burial and funeral. Eddie seemed to have recovered, and proudly told his tale of how brave he'd been with the bad guys. Mia could attest to that.

The board had delivered the decision to implement Mia's software program. The process was moving forward rapidly, and remedial students had access to it over the summer. Iris and Griffen were managing the company, while Mia took a few weeks off.

The media exploded with news of Mia's abduction. The tale was told repeatedly with many embellishments, though the real story was riveting enough. Mia still couldn't believe that she'd survived. The fans were in a frenzy, and she was touched by all the support.

The threat was gone, and Mia had a chance to recover. It would take a while to heal, mentally and physically. Ryker had been with her every second, attentive and caring. She loved him more than she thought possible.

Ryker stopped swinging and came over to stand in front of her. He pulled Mia up and wrapped his arms around her. She looked into his loving eyes. "You've made my heart whole again," he said, then touched her cheek.

Mia couldn't begin to tell him what he meant to her.

Ryker kissed her gently then said, "Let me love and protect you. That's my greatest desire."

"I love you with all my heart," Mia said, "and I think I've proven that I certainly need protecting."

Then Ryker pulled a tiny box from his pocket and opened it. A diamond engagement ring sparkled in the sunlight. "Marry me," Ryker said, then dropped to one knee. "I promise to honor your love."

Mia choked up. She hadn't had a family, or a man she could trust. Her heart swelled with joy and a tear rolled down her cheek. "Yes...yes, I'll marry you."

Ryker stood and put the ring on her finger. Then he kissed her deeply, before looking into her eyes.

"With one condition," Mia said.

"You name it."

"For our honeymoon, we don't go to Europe, especially not the Pyrenees."

"*That* I can do." Ryker lifted her hand and kissed the diamond on her finger. Then he pulled her close for a passionate kiss.

Turn the page for a sneak peek inside:

Lethal Peril (Stealth Security Book 2)

Available now!

LETHAL PERIL

Stealth Security

Emily Jane Trent

CHAPTER 1

Elizabeth Marie Foster had been born into wealth with the apparent enviable advantages. It wasn't that she lacked gratitude for her fortune, but more that she'd witnessed the darker side of money and control.

Her father insisted on calling her Elizabeth, but she preferred Beth. She wasn't some snooty heiress who commanded awe from the masses—quite the opposite. She was a rebel and had been from the time she was a young girl.

Behaving properly and dressing to impress were trappings that boxed her in. At the age of twenty-eight, Beth already had a long list of offenses. Not one of them was noteworthy, taken on its own. But viewed as a whole, the acts had given her a reputation for causing trouble.

Not that Beth cared. She preferred to live on the fringes, to ignore demands, and to be her own woman. Although she hadn't quite figured out what that was, it definitely *was not* being the woman that she was expected to be—but one of her own design.

Elizabeth, the only daughter of shipping

magnate Stephen Charles Foster, breathed in the brisk Manhattan air. The walk through Central Park had been invigorating. She glanced back at the fall colors of the leaves, dangling from the trees and scattered across the lawn. As a young girl, she'd spent time at the park, frequently in the company of her mother.

But her mother had passed away, a victim of cancer, long before Elizabeth graduated from grade school. To this day she missed her, and the loveliness of the park was a stark reminder of the motherly love that had been taken away much too soon.

Turning toward the street, she focused on her plans for Saturday. She cherished her liberty from the confines of an office, and embraced the relief of being away from her stifling life. In his generosity, her father had given her a job, doing accounting for Foster International. Despite her assumed untrustworthiness, he had faith in her.

Thus Stephen Foster had entrusted his billion-dollar baby to her, allowing her to work in bookkeeping, as part of his accounting team. Not her preference at all. But she hadn't had the heart to reject his loving gesture. Of any family member, apart from her dearly departed mother, Elizabeth loved her father most. More accurately, she adored him.

Reflection on her employment at Foster

tightened her chest and brought tears to her eyes. She brushed them away with the back of her hand. This was no time for sentimentality. What she'd been accused of was beyond the realm of possibility. Yet it was so damn easy for others to believe it of her.

Elizabeth stuffed her hands in her pockets and strode toward Fifth Avenue to catch the subway. She'd remembered to wear a jacket, but not her gloves. Her hand closed around a tiny sketchbook that she carried with her. Drawing caricatures was her hobby, so in the park she'd sketched a couple of the tourists. Such were simple to spot, since they gawked at the scenery—something a New Yorker was not prone to do.

The walk from Central Park to the metro station was short, so didn't require taking a cab. Elizabeth far preferred walking, in any case. She rarely opted to ride in the family limo, as it was pretentious and claustrophobic. Pedestrians filled the sidewalk, confirmation that she wasn't alone in her choice to walk instead of ride.

Up ahead, her friend waved both hands in a joyful frenzy, most likely pleased to be out of the office also. Amanda Moreau waited by the subway station, waving her arm for Elizabeth to hurry up. Shopping held an allure for her friend, not that Elizabeth objected. She found plenty to add to her wardrobe during their outings.

While hanging around the newsroom at one of the small daily papers, Elizabeth had recently met Amanda. The friendship had begun with little effort, since they had much in common—especially a sharply condescending attitude toward politics and the crimes of the wealthy.

Elizabeth drew cartoons derived from her observations, satires on political absurdities, while Amanda wrote scathing editorials on similar topics. But their friendship wasn't limited to the newsroom. In the months since Elizabeth had found her new friend, she'd agreed to various lunches and shopping sprees.

"Hey, Amanda, sorry I'm a little late. I should have picked up my pace in the park."

"Let me guess. You were sketching and lost track of time?"

Elizabeth raised her hands. "Guilty as charged."

Amanda looked her over, then grinned. "You wore that great jacket. I'm jealous. Turn around."

Elizabeth spun in a half-turn, and Amanda pulled on the hem of the bomber jacket. It was pink with black cuffs and hem. On the back was a striking logo, a symbol that had become a trademark of sorts.

"I love this thing," Amanda said. "The eagle on the back is just so...spectacular. He's magnificent outlined in rhinestones."

Slipping off her black leather jacket, Amanda grinned. She dropped her purse to the sidewalk between her feet and reached out her arms. "Okay...trade. I want to trade...just for today."

Elizabeth laughed. "Sure, why not?" The jacket was silk, a designer fashion personalized with the unique logo. The stylized eagle represented individual freedom, and served as a symbol of Elizabeth's art. She slipped her sketchbook, phone, and wallet from the pockets, then handed over the treasured garment.

Amanda put on the shiny jacket and Elizabeth donned the leather one, slipping her items into the pockets. Interests weren't all she had in common with her friend. Amanda was barely five feet two, the same as she, with a similarly small build. And the petite journalist's hairstyle was a copycat of Elizabeth's punk look—buzzed around the left ear, long on the right side, with some stray tendrils at the neckline. And her friend had a row of piercings along the curve of one ear, matching hers. Elizabeth couldn't claim credit for that, since Amanda had worn tiny hoops on that ear when she'd met her.

The identical black hair finished the look. Amanda hefted the strap of her purse over one shoulder, then motioned toward the entrance. "Shall we?"

The subway gave Elizabeth the creeps. It

wasn't the safest way to travel, but she refused to wimp out. After all, thousands of commuters rode the trains each day, so she could too. The stench of the underground and the graffiti magnified the unsettling atmosphere of public transportation.

Crowds parted and moved toward their individual destinations. "We can get off at Madison Avenue," Amanda said, "exit near Calvin Klein."

"I need some new jeans," Elizabeth said. "What you looking for?"

"Hermès has a special on shoes. Maybe I can find a pair to match the bag I snagged last time."

A group of guys bumped into Amanda, knocking her into Elizabeth, but didn't acknowledge the collision. Dressed in low-hanging baggy jeans and sloppy shirts, not one of them could have been over the age of sixteen—some high school kids, hanging out.

A tall, bulky dude leered at Elizabeth, and she gave him the stink-eye. *Asshole.* Sticking close to Amanda, parting the sea of people with an outstretched hand, Elizabeth threaded her way toward the waiting area. The station was busy, and throngs of people pushed them off course.

"Sheesh, we should have taken a taxi," Amanda said.

Elizabeth caught sight of a man she had noticed earlier, near the entrance. Unlike the other commuters, he focused on Amanda and pushed people aside, coming toward her. The fleeting thought that maybe he admired the jacket vanished when he made a beeline in her direction.

"Amanda, that guy is following us."

"Who?"

"Don't look, just keep moving." Elizabeth grabbed her arm and dragged her forward through a break in the crowd. "He's some weirdo."

But it seemed there was more to it. The man wore sunglasses and a ball cap. He was broad-shouldered and appeared intent on something. Elizabeth feared it was Amanda, or maybe both of them. But what idiot would kidnap two women in the middle of a subway station? Then again, this was New York.

Elizabeth moved faster. The waiting area was near; she could see it. Glancing back was a mistake. The pursuer was just a few people behind. Her heart pounded. It made no sense. Some strange guy wouldn't grab them in broad daylight, or in this dark subway tunnel filled with witnesses.

"We're late," Amanda said.

As if to confirm that fact, a mass of people pushed toward the edge, leaning to see if the train was coming. The noise of the subway train drowned out conversation, yet the roar of voices of the waiting passengers blended with its reverberating sound.

"We better get up there," Elizabeth said, nearly shouting. In the same instant, a frantic crowd swept her friend away, like driftwood at sea. One minute they were together inching ahead, and the next, Amanda was carried forward into the crowd.

Giddy with the fight for the subway train, Elizabeth clung to the assurance that if Amanda got in first that she'd save her a seat. Then the man in the ball cap broke free of the mass of people, like some bizarre superhero, who was stronger than anyone near him.

Elizabeth couldn't breathe. The air was stifling and the crowd suffocated her. Then the scary man was only inches from her friend. "Amanda," she screamed, but it was futile. Her friend didn't look back.

The ground rumbled as the heavy train approached. Elizabeth stood tall to look over the crowd; Amanda was at the edge, close to the rails. The strange man was next to her, as if he might say something. Then he lurched against Amanda, knocking her into open space and onto the tracks.

Elizabeth screamed and thrust her hands into her hair. It was a nightmare. It had to be. Soon she'd wake up to find that she was still in her bed, away from the horror she'd witnessed. Her heart sank to her feet, and on trembling legs she staggered forward.

The crowd had backed away, leaving an open path. Frantically, Elizabeth made her way to the scene and looked down at the tracks, before she thought better of it. Tears streamed down her cheeks, and she hugged her arms around her waist, rocking back and forth as she wailed with distress.

Amanda was dead.

Elizabeth turned and moved away from the disaster, hardly able to see through her burning tears. She bumped into a row of wooden seating. Instead of sitting down, she slumped against the wall and slid to the floor, shivering uncontrollably. Images of the incident flashed through her mind. The man had pushed Amanda. She'd witnessed it; seen it with her own eyes.

Looking up through blurry vision, Elizabeth couldn't pick the man out of the crowd. *Gone. He's gone.* Shock engulfed her, rendering her speechless and preventing her from moving. She reeled with confusion. *Why?* It was so senseless.

Elizabeth put her hands over her eyes and sobbed. Amanda was gone. It was a tragedy, one that couldn't be undone. Confusion addled her brain. She scanned her memory, trying to get a grip on what had transpired, but was unable to sift out the truth.

Why would anyone want to kill Amanda?

*****

A cacophony of voices and people moving about drew her attention. Elizabeth had to do something, tell someone. Numbed by the loss of her friend, she stood on shaky legs and returned to the rails, having no concept of how long it had been since the accident.

The police were there, questioning a few people. The crowd had noticeably thinned. She put her hand on the arm of a cop holding a walkie-talkie. He looked down at her and frowned. "Did you see what happened? Did you know the deceased?"

Tears rolled down Elizabeth's cheeks. "She was my friend. We were together. Her name is Amanda Moreau. She's...*was* a journalist."

The cop lowered his radio and gave her his attention. "Did she jump?"

Elizabeth shook her head. "No. No."

"Was she drunk or high?"

"She was...*murdered*."

The cop didn't seem alarmed. "Do you realize what you're saying?

His disbelief cut through the haze, stirring anger. "Yes. I do. I saw it happen. A man pushed her."

"And what's your name?"

"Elizabeth Foster."

"Lady, I don't mean to be disrespectful, but do

you know there have been over eighty deaths this year alone, from people falling on the metro tracks? Most are suicides, the rest are accidents, as a result of intoxication with alcohol or cocaine."

Elizabeth glared at him, irritated by his reciting of statistics. "I don't care. I'm telling you that my friend was pushed."

"We've spoken to the motorman. He didn't see anyone else. What he did see was a woman's body plummet to the tracks in front of the train, so he hit the emergency brake and laid on the horn."

The denial of her allegation infuriated her.

The cop's gaze hardened. "So where have you been, then...if you saw it happen?"

"I was...over there." Elizabeth waved her hand toward the wall. "I couldn't get to her. I couldn't...do anything."

After a moment, the cop huffed. "I need you to give a statement, then. Let's go down to the station."

He proceeded to escort her to his vehicle, and, considering his attitude, it was surprising that he didn't cuff her. The cop talked on his radio, letting the station know he was coming in. Elizabeth rested her head against the seat and stared up at nothing.

This was all a horrible mistake. It had to be. She'd known Amanda. The woman didn't have enemies. She'd worked an entry-level position at a daily paper. Not the stuff notoriety was made from. She hadn't developed the kind of career that could get her killed.

Elizabeth struggled to recall if Amanda had mentioned anyone in her private life who posed a threat, but came up blank. Amanda dated but wasn't hooked up with anyone. There was no man who'd abused her or wished her harm. Not that she'd spoken of.

When Elizabeth closed her eyes, the image of her silk bomber jacket filled her mind. Her gut twisted as she recalled the pink, sparkly garment that Amanda had worn to her death. Elizabeth's eyes flew open. *Oh my God. Could that be?*

Spotting Elizabeth would have been an easy task, even for a man who hadn't seen her before. The logo on the jacket was a giveaway. Even those who hadn't seen Elizabeth's cartoon drawings recognized the logo. That vector image of an eagle was plastered in news media, on publications that printed her art, and, most prominently, on her jacket.

Amanda had looked enough like Elizabeth to be her twin. From the back: same height, hair color, and style. Both had on jeans and boots. Yet there was one significant difference, the one thing that set them apart—the logo jacket.

Her friend may not have had enemies, but

Elizabeth sure did. Playing the role of the rebel hadn't endeared others to her, even her own family. And recently, she'd been on the outs with them. Yet she couldn't envision it was sufficient motive to kill.

But the alternative, that the killer had been after Amanda, didn't ring true. It was more likely, as absurd as it seemed, that the killer had been sent to take out Elizabeth. She shuddered. Her family was wealthy, rich from billions handed down for many generations. Old money garnered from the lucrative shipping industry.

There was no doubt that her family had the resources to remove any person that got in the way of finance. But murder? That was beyond any improprieties she had knowledge of. Yet could she really put it past them?

And who would commit murder...who was that desperate? Certainly not her father. But other than him, Elizabeth considered any family member capable of such a deed. Not personally, of course. But for the right price, a killer could have been hired. A tingle of fear ran up her spine. However incredible, she was unable to brush aside her suspicions.

Elizabeth sat up. The cop glanced over at her, then turned into the parking lot. She needed her lawyer; things were out of hand. Pulling her phone from the pocket of the leather jacket, she dialed the family attorney.

"Who are you calling?"

"My attorney," Elizabeth said. "I'll have him meet me at the station. You'll just have to wait until he arrives."

The cop clenched his jaw.

"I'm not under arrest, am I?"

"It's just an interview." The cop pulled into an open parking space. "You're the one that's so anxious to turn this into a murder investigation."

"Hardly." Elizabeth glared at him. "But a friend of mine died. I'm not about to keep quiet."

*****

The police station was no more welcoming than the subway had been. Thomas Stapleton, attorney-at-law, had represented the family for as long as Elizabeth could recall. He was a welcome sight, striding toward her, sporting an expensive leather briefcase. Even on such short notice, he'd managed to arrive in a tailored suit.

"What can I do for you, Elizabeth?"

Thomas didn't seem all that surprised to find her at the police station. He had been around so long he was like part of the family, thus he knew of her escapades. Yet this went far beyond her mischievous games. This was for real.

Elizabeth gave him the punch line first, letting him know that she'd witnessed a murder. He raised his brows. "We need to speak alone before you agree to an interview."

The cop reluctantly agreed to let them have an empty office, and Elizabeth proceeded to relay her version of the event. She clarified that the cop asserted the death had been an accident, and was skeptical of her claim that it had been murder.

Having heard the blow-by-blow of what had happened that morning, Thomas expressed concern over her emotional state. After her assurance that she was all right for now, he leaned back in his chair. "I can't advise you to give a statement at this time. The situation is quite volatile. If you are to be interviewed, it should be in a formal setting where I am present. I'd like to look over all the facts, and the police investigation, before such an interview takes place."

It wasn't lost on Elizabeth that her attorney's first priority was the family's reputation. Any story that involved Foster International, or any member of the Foster family, spread like wildfire. Mere rumors turned into headlines overnight. An incident involving alleged murder would spiral out of control.

Elizabeth studied her attorney. "So I can count on you to keep this quiet?"

"What do you mean by quiet?"

"I'd rather you not tell anyone just yet."

"I'm not sure that's a good idea. Your uncle

should be told. He will be furious if something like this is withheld from him."

Elizabeth shrugged. Martin Foster, her father's younger brother, would hit the roof when he heard about this. But she needed time. "Yes, but my uncle knows me." She gave Thomas an impish grin. "He won't blame you. I promise not to tell him that I called you to the station. I'll take the fallout for any upset."

"Elizabeth…"

"Really, I promise. So please, just for a day or two, until I can figure things out. And it's a given that you won't relay any of this to my father either." That last stipulation likely wasn't necessary, but she had to make sure.

Thomas shook his head. "Against my better judgment. But I need your agreement not to speak to the authorities unless I'm present."

"Deal."

"You realize that your uncle will find out anyway, as well as your father?"

"But not immediately. And when it does come up—because I'm sure the police won't keep a lid on a story like this—you can use your standard line that the family wishes to maintain their privacy."

Thomas stood and lifted his briefcase from the table. "Okay, but I insist on driving you home."

*****

Lethal Peril

Home was a three-story mansion in Manhattan, where Elizabeth had lived with her father for many years. It had five fireplaces, a basement swimming pool, and two gardens. She found no joy in the fact that she had it all to herself.

Other than the maids who came in to clean, or the maintenance man who tended to the upkeep, Elizabeth rambled through the spacious quarters quite alone. The reason saddened her, yet she was at a loss on how to make her life any different than it was.

After Thomas dropped her off, she went up to the rooftop patio to gaze at the scene below. It was one feature of the house that pleased her. Up so high, with a view of the city, Elizabeth was above it all. She often gained perspective on things while lounging on the terrace, alone with her thoughts.

She would have much preferred for her father to join her, but that was no longer possible. Only months before, the sudden onset of Alzheimer's had taken him away. For his own safety, her loving father Stephen Foster had been placed in a nursing facility with twenty-four-hour care.

Plopping into a cushy patio chair, Elizabeth looked up at the sky. It was a gorgeous shade of eggshell blue with a few wispy clouds slowly drifting, languidly progressing over the city without a care in the world. If only she could claim the same.

Until a week ago, Elizabeth had spent much of her week as an accounting department employee at Foster International, doing her part to keep the books straight. She wasn't destined to be an accountant, but her father had employed her in that department due to her talent with software and computers.

She'd grown up using computers, so it was no special talent. Or so she claimed. Yet she understood such things better than some, and she tinkered incessantly, playing around with software as a hobby. It was interesting, which was something she needed.

Yet now she'd been removed from that function and her father was locked away in a facility. Elizabeth was acutely aware of her lack of friends. It was to her disadvantage that she'd been somewhat antisocial growing up. It wasn't that she had a particular dislike of others, but more that she tended to entertain herself. Sketching her cartoons, or plunking around on computer keyboards, occupied too much of her time. Now that she was in dire straits, she suffered a pang of regret about not connecting with anyone else much sooner.

It hadn't been all bleak. Elizabeth had bonded with Amanda. On reflection, maybe she shouldn't have, as she was more and more convinced that her friend's death fell on her shoulders. She could have warned Amanda that hanging around with her could mean trouble. But in her wildest imaginings, Elizabeth hadn't dreamed such a relationship involved lethal peril.

The wind whipped across the terrace, and Elizabeth wrapped the jacket tighter around her. The transparent panels around the rooftop, intended to block the wind, were inadequate. There were heaters to handle the chill from the rapidly dropping temperature, but she couldn't muster the initiative to get up and turn them on.

With her feet on the chair, Elizabeth wrapped her arms around her legs and rested her chin on her knees. In the quiet of her rooftop respite, she dug deep for answers. Now that her father was incapacitated, her brother Kyle ran operations at the shipping company under her Uncle Martin's supervision. She had no issue with that, as she certainly didn't want the duty.

She didn't have any responsibility for medical decisions concerning her father either, as he had given power of attorney to his brother Martin. Once the illness had been diagnosed, her uncle had taken charge. Not that Elizabeth would have done anything differently. Her father was sick and needed expert care. He was better off in the facility, as he couldn't be properly cared for at home.

It didn't matter that no particular duties fell to Elizabeth. Her family had no faith in her, and hadn't for some time. Only her father gave her credit, probably more than she deserved, for her abilities. But now he barely recognized her when she visited.

There was no one to turn to. It was out of the question to go to her uncle with her dilemma. He wouldn't listen to her anyway. And her brother was well intended but naïve. The idea that he'd believe that her friend was murdered was ludicrous. He'd accuse her of imagining the whole thing.

Her friend had died, and if Elizabeth's theory was correct, the incident had some connection to past transgressions. But she had no idea what acts had been significant enough to provoke murder. Yet if the killer was after her, he would soon enough realize his error.

Her life was in danger. She'd told her attorney about the murder, but she'd kept silent about her concern that it was in some way connected to her. If she had breathed a word of that, Thomas would have insisted that she hire a bodyguard. In the past, she'd adamantly refused to be guarded like a prisoner.

Elizabeth had been safe enough in her daily life. But these were unusual circumstances. Hiring a bodyguard wasn't such a bad idea. The more she pondered it, the more it seemed like the right thing to do. She was in a tight spot and needed help.

There was no one she could turn to—except for *one man*. Elizabeth pulled out her phone and punched the button for the airlines, before she could change her mind. She booked an early flight for Los Angeles, then went downstairs to pack.

ABOUT THE AUTHOR

Emily Jane Trent writes romantic suspense and steamy romances about characters you'll get to know and love. If you are a fan of stories with a heroine that's got spunk and a hunk of a hero that you'd like to take home with you, these stories are what you're looking for. Emily's romantic tales will let you escape into a fantasy – and you won't want it to end - ever.

Emily would be pleased to have you join her VIP reader group by signing up for her newsletter. You'll be notified of any deals, specials, and upcoming releases!

EmilyJaneTrent.com/VIP-Readers

Made in the USA
Monee, IL
21 December 2019